"Julia," Tre
"Let Me In."

"Is that an order from the boss?" she asked lightly.

"If it needs to be, darlin'."

His soft words and Southern drawl were enough enticement. She moved away from the door and he made his way inside. He glanced at the large bouquet on the sofa table.

"You do flowers well," she said. "You're a talented man."

He arched a brow and devoured her with a look. "You know I am." He grabbed at her robe sash.

Julia closed her eyes. "Trent."

"You're naked under this robe, Julia. And in my arms."

"I work for you now," she said, announcing the obvious.

"It's after hours."

"It doesn't feel right."

A low ripple of laughter escaped Trent's throat. "Don't lie."

Dear Reader,

I love cowboys! I guess I always have, so when Texan-born, Stetson-wearing Trent Tyler appeared in his brother's story, *The Corporate Raider's Revenge,* I had no option but to make him a Western man with all the trimmings. The rugged, sexy millionaire heading up Arizona's Tempest West Hotel soon became my *Five-Star Cowboy,* and the SUITE SECRETS series took shape.

Set against the backdrop of stunning wild sunsets and natural lakes at Crimson Canyon, *Five-Star Cowboy* is the first of a trilogy, and all are set in some of my favorite locations. This first is set in Arizona. New Orleans is the backdrop for *Do Not Disturb Until Christmas*—out this November. And the final book will be set in Hawaii. I've traveled to each of these locales for research as well as pleasure. I know…a tough job, but someone has to do it, right?

I hope you fall in love with Trent and Julia from page one, as I did. Once you get past the deceptions you'll find the pair remarkable and really quite likable. Keep your eyes peeled for Cody Landon and Brock Tyler, too. Their stories won't be far behind!

Happy reading!

Charlene Sands

CHARLENE SANDS

FIVE-STAR COWBOY

Silhouette® Desire

Published by Silhouette Books
America's Publisher of Contemporary Romance

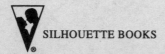 SILHOUETTE BOOKS

ISBN-13: 978-0-373-76889-9
ISBN-10:   0-373-76889-3

FIVE-STAR COWBOY

Recent books by Charlene Sands

Silhouette Desire

Bunking Down with the Boss #1746
Fortune's Vengeful Groom #1783
Between the CEO's Sheets #1805
The Corporate Raider's Revenge #1848
*Five-Star Cowboy #1889

Harlequin Historical

The Courting of Widow Shaw #710
Renegade Wife #789
Abducted at the Altar #816

*Suite Secrets

CHARLENE SANDS

resides in Southern California with her husband, Don—her high school sweetheart and best friend. They boast proudly that their children, Jason and Nikki, have earned their college degrees. The "empty nesters" now have two cats that have taken over the house. Charlene's love of the American West, both present and past, stems from storytelling days with her imaginative father—sparking a passion for a good story and her desire to write romance. She's written more than twenty romances and is the recipient of a 2006 National Readers' Choice Award and, the 2007 CataRomance Reviewer's Choice Award, with nominations for numerous other awards. When not writing, she enjoys sunny California days, Pacific beaches and sitting down with a good book.

Charlene invites you to visit her Web site at www.charlenesands.com to enter her contests and see what's new. She blogs regularly on the all-western site at www.petticoatsandpistols.com and you can also find her at www.myspace.com/charlenesands.

To my wonderful son Jason and his sweet girlfriend,
Lindsay. May you always share great times,
deep respect and never-ending sports!
You both are very close to my heart.

One

"There's my miracle worker." Trent Tyler smiled as he sauntered out of the Arizona hotel's wide, high-arched front doors, his rich sexy voice doing a number on Julia Lowell already. It still amazed her that all of this belonged to Trent.

She steadied herself against the limousine that had brought her to Crimson Canyon, her breath catching in her throat seeing Trent again. She reminded herself that he was her boss now. She could no longer think of him as the man who knew how to push all her sexual buttons.

He strode over to her with a sure-and-easy gait that always attracted female eyes. As he approached, wearing crisp denim Wranglers, a black studded shirt and a western buckle that reflected the last glimmers of Arizona sunlight, he put a finger to his Stetson in a polite tip.

"We're going to need a miracle, Trent."

"I've got faith in you, darlin'. You'll pull it off." He turned to the limo driver. "Put Miss Lowell's gear in her room, Kirby."

"Will do, Mr. Tyler."

Once the driver took her luggage away, Julia stared into Trent's dark eyes and reminded herself of their professional relationship now. She'd handed him her full resume in person that told him of her accomplishments. A master's degree in business and landing a job fresh out of graduate school as an executive in the biggest marketing firm in Los Angeles had been enough of a recommendation for him. She was Laney's best friend and could be trusted, he'd said when he'd offered her the job.

They'd met months ago when Laney had married Trent's brother Evan. Sparks had flown immediately, the tall, handsome Texan catching Julia's eye from the get-go. Directly after the wedding, Julia and Trent had had a wild weekend affair and she'd never heard from him again.

Until two weeks ago. When he'd shown up on her doorstep in Los Angeles with flowers, champagne and an apology for not calling.

Trent lifted his lips in a devilish grin. "You look gorgeous."

She would have blushed if her olive skin tone allowed it. How could she forget those hot sizzling nights spent in Trent's arms? They'd nearly combusted and gone up in a big puff of smoke. How could she forget the way he'd whisper her name right before her body shattered into a thousand pieces?

She had debated her spontaneous decision to accept this marketing position a dozen times over the past weeks. Trent had the markings of a confirmed bachelor who was dedicated to his project. He'd made it clear he wasn't interested in a relationship. Tempest West was his priority, claiming all of his time and energy. Yet every time they'd been together, at his brother's wedding and then just weeks ago, they couldn't keep their hands off each other.

Her friend Laney had always insisted that the right woman could sway any man and that she and Evan were living proof of that. Julia feared she was in too deep already. Trent affected her in ways she'd never felt before and when she looked at him, she envisioned a real life with him, and a family.

Trent pulled her near, closing his hands around her waist, and bent his head, his hat brim shadowing his eyes. "It's good to see you."

Be strong, Julia.

She sucked oxygen deep into her lungs and set her hands on his chest. As she felt his strength through the fabric of his shirt, her resistance faded like the last crimson blaze of sunshine.

Trent smiled and leaned in for a kiss.

She gazed at his mouth right before his lips touched

hers briefly. Sensations rippled wickedly through her body. The kiss ended quickly, but the impact of his sensual mouth caressing hers remained. Unable to meet his eyes, she peered at his throat. "Maybe, uh, we need some ground rules, Trent."

"I agree," he said instantly. Then he put his arm around her waist and guided her toward the front door. "I'll take you to your room. Let you settle in. We'll have dinner in an hour and talk."

He agreed…just like that? Julia slanted him a glance. He didn't flinch. Maybe he'd realized that once she'd become his employee, and she'd be living on the premises as part of her contract, they'd have to draw a line in the desert sand.

"Okay." Was she disappointed or relieved?

A second later, she decided she was both.

Trent dived into his work at his hotel the same way he did everything else in his life, giving one hundred percent. He could be ruthless at times, tenacious when necessary and as immovable as rock when he believed he was right about something.

He was right about Tempest West. Down in his bones, he knew he'd make a success of it. He wasn't cut out to work in a big city like his brother Evan or schmooze with an elite crowd like Brock, the party animal of the Tyler brothers. So the declaration he'd made had fallen easily from his lips—"Tempest West will make more money than any new Tempest Hotel in its first year of operation."

Brock, never one to shy away from a dare, took the bet without blinking. He was scheduled to open a new Tempest Hotel on Maui and Evan had been hauled into the challenge to referee. It was reminiscent of their youth, when the two headstrong boys would compete and the oldest would make sure they both played fair. Evan and Brock both thought Trent didn't stand a chance in hell of winning.

Tempest West's rustic, western-themed hotel called to a different clientele and didn't fit in with the smooth, sleek style of the other well-established hotels in their chain. Trent had sunk his own money into his dream hotel. Tempest West was his, and his alone. He'd put his whole heart into it and now his reputation, pride and ego were on the line.

Tempest West had opened with flair, but in the few months since, occupancy rates had dropped off, meaning they were only making a marginal profit. Trent had fired his last marketing VP. He'd needed a fresh approach, someone with a new vision. He'd needed Julia Lowell.

And he'd done everything in his power to get her here.

With his arm loosely on her waist, Trent steered Julia toward the massive lobby of the hotel. "This is my favorite spot inside the hotel."

Julia scanned the surroundings with a look of sheer wonder in her eyes. "The pictures in your brochures don't come close. This is amazing, Trent."

"Amazing's a good description." He couldn't deny it.

He'd spared no cost to bring the allure and amazing Crimson Canyon sunsets into the lobby. Tall, expansive windows banked the entire west wall and brought the beauty of the outside, inside. Majestic red rock mountains concealed the lower edge of the setting sun now. Golden light put a glow onto the land Trent owned, dotted with cottonwoods in the distance.

He put one hand on Julia's shoulder and pointed with the other. "See way out where your eyes skitter across a sea of blue? That's Destiny Lake. There's a legend that goes along with that name. I'll tell you about it someday."

"Trent, this is wonderful. You've brought the west here, with the furnishings and stone fireplaces. It doesn't feel like a hotel lobby, but a warm and friendly greeting place."

Trent squeezed her shoulder. "I want you to see it all—the land, the lake, the riding stables. There's a modern-day bunkhouse where the wranglers stay. Tomorrow I'll take you on the nickel tour."

Julia's satisfied smile made his groin twitch. He'd put that look on her face before when she'd fallen into his arms after a powerful orgasm. Then she'd curled herself into him and he'd held her until sleep claimed them.

She had a slender body, gorgeous legs, pretty light green eyes and dark chestnut hair, but it was more with Julia. The sex between them was the best he'd ever had. When they were together, they detonated like dynamite.

He'd been ruthless in his quest to get her to Tempest West and felt a twinge of guilt, but not enough to tell her the truth and jeopardize the hotel's success. As long as she didn't find out he'd orchestrated her losing the Bridges Restaurant account in New York to bring her here, he'd be in the clear. He'd do whatever necessary to keep her in the dark about his high-handed manipulation. He couldn't afford for her to find out.

Trent wanted her in the boardroom and in his bedroom. She'd turn the hotel vacancy rate around, helping him prove to his brothers Tempest West could keep up with the other hotels, while he and Julia filled their unquenchable thirst for each other.

Both stood to gain.

"I'll come get you in an hour. We'll have dinner," he said as he guided her from the lobby to the small open-air elevator that would take her to a private suite on the third floor. Reaching into his pocket, he pulled out a key card and set it into her palm. Stroking his thumb over her fingers reminded him of breathless whispers and nights of desperate, crazy sex. "I'd come in with you, but then I doubt you'd get the rest you need."

She shook her head. "Trent."

He let her go and glanced down her long legs to her red-sandaled feet. He'd never forget making love to her, demanding that she take everything off *but* those sexy shoes. "You wore them."

Julia's eyes flickered. "They match my outfit." She didn't pretend not to catch his meaning and that brought his appraisal of her up a notch.

He sent a smile. "Sure do like a woman with good fashion sense."

* * *

Julia kicked off her sandals the minute she entered the room. She took a big breath, filled her lungs and blocked out the memory flash those sandals evoked. She walked over to a beautiful arrangement of flowers waiting for her on the sofa table and read the card's greeting.

Once she noticed her surroundings though, her mind shifted into business mode. The suite fulfilled all of the expectations she'd envisioned for Tempest West.

Rustic with class and style. Luxurious with understated amenities. Simple, yet elegant in design. Trent had spared no expense and took great pride in the décor, the views and the unpretentious use of space. She walked the length of the suite to look out the rectangular wide-paned window to the view below.

The hotel itself was only three stories high but the heart of the grounds was in the one-story attached cottage suites that circled out in a horseshoe shape from the main hotel in both directions and overlooked the stables, the lake and the canyon beyond.

"You've outdone yourself with this place, Trent," she murmured, a smile emerging. Everything Trent did, he did with positive enthusiasm, giving of himself one hundred percent. Julia had the erotic memories to prove it.

She walked into the spacious bedroom and unpacked her clothes, placing her casual attire in the armoire drawers and hanging up her work clothes in the walk-in closet. Next, she strolled to the double oak doors that led to a large private balcony and flipped open her cell phone, hit auto-dial and waited. After the second ring, her father picked up. "Hi, Daddy," she said. "I'm here, safe and sound."

"That's good, sweetheart. I appreciate the call."

Julia was nearly thirty years old but she didn't mind checking in with her dad. Her mother had died two years ago and she knew her father was extremely lonely. They'd always been close and although she'd been terribly disappointed when she'd lost the contract she'd vied for with a national restaurant chain, she'd witnessed relief on her father's face when she'd told him she wouldn't be moving to New York after all.

A few days later, Trent had shown up on her doorstep in Los Angeles apologizing for not keeping in contact with her after their weekend affair after Evan and Laney's wedding. Flowers, champagne and a night in Trent's arms had gone a long way in consoling her, especially after the ego hit she'd taken losing the Bridges account. Before long, she'd had to break the news to her dad that she'd be moving to Arizona to work for Trent Tyler. He'd made her an ideal offer that she couldn't justify refusing.

"So, how is Tempest West?"

"Dad, it's stunning. The place has so much to offer. I think I'll be able to help Trent make it a destination for the elite."

"I know you will. You've got my genes."

She laughed as she was reminded of her father's

success in the banking industry. He had a good head for business and apparently, she'd taken after him. "I know I do. You gave me smarts and I intend to use them here."

"That's my girl," he said and once the conversation ended, Julia stripped out of her clothes and turned the spigot to Hot in the oversize, tiled shower. She made quick work of stepping in, soaping up and rinsing off. Minutes later, she donned a fluffy white robe from the vanity closet and hugged herself around the middle, enjoying the lush feel of soft cotton against her skin. She flopped onto the king-size four-poster bed, seeking a little rest before dinner, and promptly fell asleep.

"Julia. It's Trent. Are you in there?"

Julia rose, disoriented for a moment when she heard Trent's voice calling her from behind the suite's double doors. The hour had flown by. She'd overslept.

"Yes, yes. I'm here, Trent," she called out, tying the robe's sash tightly around her waist and padding over to the front door.

Julia unlocked the door and opened it a few inches, making eye contact with Trent. "Sorry," she said, "I took a nap and lost track of time."

"You're not letting me in?"

"I'm not dressed. I'll meet you—"

"Julia," he groaned, "let me in."

"Is that an order from the boss?" she asked lightly.

"If it needs to be, darlin'."

His soft words and southern drawl were enough enticement. She moved away from the door and he made his way inside.

Naked underneath, she felt self-conscious in the big robe with only her head poking out of the top and red-polished toenails visible at the bottom. Trent, on the other hand, looked like a million bucks, wearing black jeans, a white western shirt, a pair of shiny boots and a charming smile.

Trent glanced at the large bouquet of deep crimson stargazers sitting in a vase on the sofa table and nodded his approval. The "We'll do great things together" card, signed by Trent, had sent a surge of warmth radiating through her body when she'd read the sentiment. "You do flowers well."

Trent smiled again. "I can tie my shoelaces and cut my own meat pretty darn good, too."

"You're a talented man."

He arched a brow and devoured her with a look. "You know I am."

The warmth stealing into her body turned to steamy sizzle. It had always been like that with Trent. Even the most innocent conversation could turn to innuendo quickly. And innuendo usually led to a fulfilling night of lust.

"I'd better get dressed," she said, turning away.

Trent grabbed at her robe sash and the traitorous tie unfastened easily. As he stood behind her, his arms came around and his hands found the separation of the parted robe easily. He stroked her bare belly, generating pulse-pounding electricity. "Hmm, I thought so."

Julia closed her eyes. "Trent."

"You're naked under this robe, Julia. And in my arms." He nibbled on her throat, setting her nerves on fire.

She stood with her back to him, allowing his caresses. His hands glided upward, teasing the underside of her breasts. "I work for you now," she said, announcing the obvious.

"It's after hours."

"It doesn't feel right."

A low ripple of laughter escaped his throat. "Don't lie."

She had lied…to him. Oh, God, how she wanted him. But she'd lied to herself, too, because keeping a professional distance from her boss aside, Julia wanted more from Trent. She wanted what Laney and Evan had. She wanted true love. She yearned for a family. Her clock was ticking—at twenty-nine, she wasn't getting any younger. She'd started out as a career woman, but Julia was too much of a romantic not to want a future with a loving man beside her. She'd made one mistake already with a coworker at Powers International. She'd almost lost her job and her reputation, with a power-hungry man who'd used her to get ahead. She'd long gotten over Jerry Baker, but the sting of his betrayal stayed with her. Now, she had her own company—Lowell Strategies—but her reputation was still on the line. And so was her heart.

Trent separated the folds of the robe farther and

stroked her from breasts to hips with hands on either side of her torso, his fingers sliding up and down like a skilled guitarist strumming an erotic rhythm.

"You can walk away from me and get dressed," he murmured in her ear, "or I can take this robe off you."

Julia was running out of excuses. "We need to talk about the hotel." He'd been adamant about starting in a new direction as soon as possible. Trent made no bones about how important this project was to him. He'd summoned her to Tempest West immediately to start working on a new promotion for the hotel.

"We will. After."

He pressed his mouth to her throat and her skin prickled from the intimate touch of his lips. Trent was so darn good at seduction. She knew what *after* meant and she wasn't sure she could deny him.

His cell phone rang and he cursed. Releasing her, he stepped away. "Damn. I have to get this."

Julia sighed with relief and slipped away from Trent, heading for her bedroom. She made sure to close the door and lock it. Then she leaned her head back and took some calming breaths as she overheard Trent issuing orders to whomever was on the other end of the phone.

She slipped out of her robe and dressed in haste.

It wouldn't do her an ounce of good to fall in love with her boss. Especially since she was halfway there already.

Two

"Nice escape earlier," Trent said with a grin, leaning forward in his chair and pouring Julia a flute of champagne.

She watched the bubbly liquid rise up in the angled glass before casting her gaze his way. After the phone call that interrupted them in her suite, she'd come out fully dressed in a conservative black dress, holding her briefcase and claiming starvation. Trent hadn't pressed her, but whisked her off to a private dining room within the hotel's main restaurant, the Canyon Room.

"It was necessary…for my equilibrium." That much was true. Trent always made her dizzy, but no more so than now seeing him so comfortable and at ease in his own element.

"Well, then…I guess I'd better make sure you're well nourished."

Their eyes connected for a moment then he lifted his glass. "To you, Julia. Thank you for coming here and saving my butt."

Julia smiled and touched her glass to his. "I haven't saved anything yet."

She sipped her champagne, savoring the cool bubbly as the liquid slid down her throat.

"You will," he countered. "I checked out your track record. In less than a year, you turned the Fitness Fanatics Gym around. It was a dying enterprise. Only wannabe bodybuilders and weight trainers joined. Now it's family-oriented—parents bring their children with them. Kids learn good eating habits, self-esteem *and* keep physically fit. Developing Fit Fans For Kids was brilliant."

Julia accepted his praise without modesty. She'd worked extremely hard on that project. "Thank you. I'm still a little bit in awe at how well that turned out. The project exceeded my expectations." She slanted her head somewhat and searched his face, impressed that Trent went the extra mile to learn about her recent project. "You checked me out?"

"Many times, darlin'. And you've always exceeded my expectations."

Julia melted at the way his dark eyes flickered when he spoke the endearment. She took another sip of champagne, thinking about how his rough hands had touched her skin tenderly minutes ago and how his fingers had grazed the underside of her breasts.

Trent was a force to be reckoned with.

"You know that's not what I meant."

He smiled before sipping champagne. "I know. But I also know we're great together. I haven't been with another woman since we met."

Julia swallowed and cleared her throat. They'd never spoken of commitment. They'd had a fling that kept on flinging, but she knew going in that Trent wasn't serious about a permanent relationship. He'd never mentioned wanting to be exclusive, but it thrilled her knowing he hadn't been with other women. It still surprised her that he expected to pick up where they left off.

"I haven't, either—been with another man."

How could she? She'd never find anyone better than Trent Tyler. Not in or out of bed.

"Okay, as long as we're straight about that," he said.

His expression told her he was as glad as she was. Granted, it had been only two weeks since he'd shown up on her doorstep bearing gifts and apologizing for taking so long to see her again. Months before, after Evan and Laney's wedding, they'd had a weekend of shameless sex that Julia would never forget.

She squirmed in her chair and changed the subject. "Have you spoken with Evan lately?"

"No. I imagine he's beside himself with the baby coming soon."

Evan was the perfect doting husband and father-to-be. Julia envied Evan and Laney's relationship and hoped to have that kind of love in her life one day. "He is. I'm hoping to surprise them both with a baby shower. Laney knows I'm throwing her a shower, but she thinks it's a few months away. You're going to have to give me some time off to make the arrangements."

Trent seemed to mull the idea over and then lifted a shoulder in a shrug. "Have the shower here."

"Here?" Julia blinked, surprised by the suggestion. "As in Tempest West, here?"

"That's right." Trent nodded. "One, I can't spare you for too long. Two, the family hasn't seen the hotel completely finished. I'd planned to bring them all out here soon anyway. Three, I can send the company jet to bring the guests here without any problem. And four, it'll make your life easier planning the thing."

"And you're all about making my life easy, right?"

Trent smiled wide and a dimple that Julia thought was extremely sexy popped out along the right side of his cheek. "That's right. I keep my employees happy."

Julia thought about the idea for a moment. "I really wanted it to be from me, Trent. I'd promised Laney this shower from the minute she became pregnant."

Trent put up both hands, surrendering with a gesture. "I won't stand in your way or say a word. Use the hotel any way you see fit."

"I'd want to pay for it."

Trent cast her a crooked grin. "We'll work something out."

Julia laughed. "You are impossible, you know that?"

He shrugged. "How many guests did you have in mind?"

Julia did a mental calculation in her head. "About forty."

Trent nodded. "Very manageable."

"Actually, Trent, it's a good idea." Julia peered out the window. Hundreds of stars illuminated the sky, casting a warm glow onto the grounds as night sounds stirred the restless quiet and a soft glimmer twinkled on the lake waters. "Laney will love this place."

Trent leaned back in his seat. "Problem solved."

"Now, on to the next." Julia lifted her briefcase onto her lap and took out a manila folder filled with her notes. "I brought along a few ideas. We can hash them out over dinner."

"Sounds good to me. I'm eager to fix what's broken here and you're the woman for the job. Work your miracles."

If only, Julia thought. She wondered if it would take a miracle for Trent to think of her as more than his hotel's savior and bedroom partner. First, she'd save the hotel and then, she'd work on the other.

After dinner, Trent introduced Julia to his staff and showed her around the interior of the hotel. Once he'd answered all of her questions about the hotel's inner workings, he led her outside and they strolled the grounds.

"I'm glad you're here, Julia. We really need a fresh

outlook," he said, taking her hand as they walked past the garden patio and away from the lights.

"I wouldn't be here if you hadn't shown up in Los Angeles when you did."

"Luck and good timing," Trent said, passing off her remark easily. He didn't want to have this conversation with her.

"I'd put all my cookies in that one basket. When I lost the Bridges account, I was devastated. It shook my confidence. I really thought I'd nailed that job."

He stopped and pulled her up against him, his hands on her hips, coaxing her closer. Distracting her wouldn't be a chore. He needed to change the subject. "Don't look back, Julia. Their loss is my gain."

When she was in Los Angeles and miles separated them, he'd put her out of his mind. But now that she was at Tempest West, Trent found himself incredibly drawn to her. Recently, all of his energy had gone into the hotel and he hadn't had time for women, until he'd met Julia and they'd connected like two lightning rods.

He stared into her eyes and bent his head for another kiss. The last one had been chaste and far too brief for his liking.

"Trent," she said, leaning back, "this isn't a good idea. We really do need to set some boundaries. I can't have your employees seeing—"

Trent looked around the grounds. "No one's out here, Julia. And they'd damned better not say anything to you."

"Someone could walk outside any second. I'm not

worried about what they might say to me, but I need their respect. I doubt I'll get that if they think I'm your main squeeze."

Trent smiled. "My main squeeze?"

Flustered, Julia waved her arms. "Or whatever they call it these days. We're all going to have to work together."

Trent backed off and put his hands on his hips, staring at her. He gave in, just for a minute, to hear what Julia had to say. "Okay. Fine."

"Thank you." She nodded, more than likely surprised he'd given in so easily. "Actually, I'm glad you agreed without an argument, because you and I…we'd never, uh…" Her gaze drifted to his lips. "We'd never be able to get work done…I mean…I don't work that way…" She slowed her speech, her eyes lingering on his mouth. "I, uh, *we* need to keep a professional distance." She looked at him with an expression of desperate longing.

Trent knew enough about Julia to know when she was hot for him. The damn feeling was mutual. "That does it," he said. He grabbed her hand and tugged her along. "C'mon. We need to talk about this in private."

"Where are you taking me?"

"Somewhere where my employees won't see a thing."

"But that's not the point," she argued feebly.

Trent wasn't buying her resistance.

"It's *exactly* the point. You want what I want, darlin'. And I'm going to see that we both get it."

Trent walked briskly, Julia just a step behind him as he tugged her along to the farthest single-dwelling cottage on the grounds. He opened the door and allowed her to enter first before closing the door, shutting out starlight. Trent blinked a few times and it took a while for his eyes to adjust.

Julia stood close. Her rapid breaths caressed his face. The soft scent of gardenias teased his nose.

He leaned against the door. "You just about had me, until you started talking about professional distance."

"Why?"

"You and I can't work together all day and not ache for each other at night. You know it's true, Julia. We can survive keeping a professional distance for about as long as we can hold our breath. Eventually, we'd have to give in. Or face the consequences."

She tilted her chin up in question. "Is that the reason you hired me, Trent?"

"I hired you because you're brilliant. You know darn well how important Tempest West is to me. If I'd wanted a woman to have sex with, I—" Trent held up on that thought. His mother hadn't raised a fool.

"You wouldn't have to hire her, right?"

Trent let go a sigh and reached for Julia. "Come here."

She walked to him with her shoulders squared, and the tension melted the minute he caressed her. He tipped her head with his thumb and kissed her lips. "I've missed you."

"You're saying all the right things," she murmured softly, wrapping her arms around his neck.

He took her in a deep kiss and pressed her closer,

until she was hip-to-hip and chest-to-chest with him. Splaying his hands along her behind, he heard the softest moans escape her lips. His senses stirred and his body grew hard and tight.

She parted her lips for him and he stroked her tongue until her breaths whooshed out. Her breasts crushed his chest. His erection strained against her belly. He hiked up her dress. His hands inched up her smooth thighs. He pushed aside the scrap of material covering her womanhood and cupped her.

"Ohh...Trent," she groaned.

After that, things got crazy. He peeled her clothes away. She ripped off his shirt. His belt and boots came next and within seconds, he lifted Julia and she wrapped her legs around his waist. She moved on him and he couldn't hold back another second. He drove himself deep inside her in one frenzied thrust and welcomed her to Tempest West, the way he'd imagined since the first moment he'd met her.

Julia skimmed her finger along Trent's jaw. He pretended to sleep, but his wide smile gave him away. They lay together in bed in a spacious room in the cottage. "Do you really think I'm brilliant?"

Trent grunted.

She leaned down and kissed him on the mouth.

"Do you?"

He opened one eye. "Fishing for compliments before dawn won't win you Brownie points."

"Do I need more Brownie points?" Julia asked, feigning innocence.

Trent rolled onto his side and pressed a finger to her nose. "Don't get cute. Any more Brownie points and you'd have to drag my lifeless body into work today."

She flopped onto her back to stare at the ceiling. Last night, they'd quaked the room and she'd ended up having three powerful orgasms along with Trent. "Why do you suppose it's like this between us?"

Trent remained silent and she didn't think he'd answer. Finally, he admitted, "Haven't a clue. It just is. Don't analyze, just enjoy."

Julia enjoyed their lovemaking too much. She'd never had casual affairs, though the one long-term relationship she'd had ended badly. She'd vowed to never get involved in the workplace again. And now, she was in bed with her boss and loving every second with him.

She turned to him with apprehension. "This could get complicated."

He leaned over and kissed her. "Not if we don't let it."

"Aside from Evan being your brother and Laney being my best friend, you're my employer. Don't you see a potential problem here?"

"No, not at all."

Was it so easy for him to dismiss the notion that if things didn't work out, they'd always have a connection through the people closest to them? Her better instincts told her to back away from this situation. But how could she? How could she give up on a ruggedly handsome, strong, intelligent man who made her tingle with just the slightest touch?

"Trent, I really meant it when I said I don't want the employees and staff to know about you and me."

He nodded, his dark eyes sincere. "Got it. Anything else?"

Julia shook her head and blew out a breath. "No, I guess that's it."

"Good." He stroked her breast, his thumb making lazy circles around the tip, bringing her a new wave of sensual heat. "Enjoy, darlin'," he said before he brought his mouth down to suckle the now-erect rosy bud.

Julia squirmed, her body responding to him without qualm or restraint. He knew every button to push and he pushed them so well. "Uh, Trent, we used up the last of the condoms last night." Between the both of them, they'd come up with three.

"Julia, relax. We're not going to need protection for what I have in mind."

Two hours later, with her body well-sated, Julia walked out of the cottage forty-five minutes after Trent, and made her way through the grounds back to her suite in the hotel. She'd showered, dressed in more casual business clothes—a tan pantsuit and ankle boots—and met with the office manager in the offices on the north side of the third floor.

"Have you seen the entire grounds yet, Miss Lowell?" Kimberly Warren asked. The office manager was pretty, blond and two years out of college.

"No, I haven't. Mr. Tyler plans on showing me around later in the day," Julia said.

"Mr. Tyler is very proud of Tempest West. We're all hoping you'll come up with something dynamic to lower our vacancy rates. We're aiming for ninety-percent occupancy."

Julia didn't show her surprise at the number Trent expected. "That's a tall order. I'm not even sure the more established Tempest Hotels manage quite so high a percentage."

"Mr. Tyler has faith in you, Miss Lowell."

"Call me Julia." She smiled at the office manager.

"Okay, Julia. Let me show you to your office. Mr. Tyler had me set you up next to his office. I guess," she said, her blue eyes looking a bit too knowing, "you two will be working closely."

Julia cleared her throat. "Yes, I suppose we will be."

"Follow me," Kimberly said. "His office is down at the end of the hall and yours is the one to the right."

Kimberly showed Julia to her office then left her to settle in. Julia glanced around, looking at the framed pictures of Tempest West from inception to completion that Trent had hung on the walls. Her desk was made of white oak and stained in light walnut, the walls were cream-colored, accented with white crown molding, and there were tall book-shelves. Other than the newest electronic technology in the room, the office maintained the western theme throughout and she noted that the softly feminine touches reminded her very much of her apartment in Los Angeles.

She spent a few minutes acquainting herself with the fax machine, the Apple computer and the intercom system. Just as she emptied the contents of her briefcase into the files in the desk drawer, Trent knocked on her door and entered.

She stood up and their eyes connected.

"Morning. Again," Trent said with a wink.

Julia glanced at the closed door and thanked goodness for small favors. He appeared fresh and well-groomed, wearing a crisp white shirt under a black jacket, a string tie and cowboy hat. He looked amazingly undaunted for a man who suggested he might need to be dragged into the office today. "Hi."

"Are you settled in?"

She looked around the room. She hadn't brought much. Most of what she needed was on her laptop or in her own head. She had good instincts and counted on them more than anything else. "I think so."

"Let Kimberly know if you need anything else."

"I'm good, Trent. The office is great."

He nodded. "Okay. Just checking." He removed his jacket and tie and set them on the back of the chair facing her desk. She stiffened, watching him casually undress in her office. Hadn't he understood her concerns last night? Before she could issue a quelling remark, he offered, "I'll take you on that nickel tour now. I want you to see Tempest West at its best."

Relieved she'd been mistaken, she nodded. Trent hadn't anything but business in mind. She'd almost forgotten about agreeing to see the acreage with him this morning. "Yes, I can't wait to see the rest of the property today."

But the devil in her knew she'd already seen the best of Tempest West last night, in Trent's arms.

Three

"Normally, we'd see the grounds on horseback, but that would take too long. Today, we're going in style." Trent opened the side passenger door of the open-air Jeep Wrangler for her.

With a smile, Julia glanced at the dusty black vehicle. She'd had quite a welcome to Tempest West yesterday, so she wasn't opposed to sitting back and letting a different kind of horsepower do the work for her today. Surely, her backside would be the better for it. "I like the way you think."

Trent lowered the brim of his hat and closed her door, then jumped into the driver's seat and put the engine in gear. "I thought you would. Hang on."

They took off down the service road and headed toward the stables. Bays and palominos and red duns came into view within a minute, the horses moving around in the corrals appearing well cared for and content.

"We own forty horses and employ eight wranglers. At any given time, there may be ten to twenty horses out for a morning or afternoon ride. There's an office in the tack room where our head wrangler, Pete Wyatt, schedules the rides."

Trent pulled to a stop and they bounded out of the Jeep. They walked to the stable entrance, which was a smaller replica of the massive high-arched entrance to the main hotel.

A man Trent's age came forward, smiling wide with an outstretched hand. "You must be Miss Julia Lowell. I'm Pete. I manage the stables. You're the lady who's gonna make sure we don't lose any in our string."

Julia shook his hand, and then slanted her gaze toward Trent. "And how will I do that?"

"By bringing in more paying guests, that's how," Pete said as if stating the obvious. "We're only working half the animals, if that. They come from good breeding, every one of them. The boys and me can only exercise them so much. They're too spry to be corralled up. Come on," he said, "I'll show you our operation."

Half an hour later, she returned with Trent to the Jeep. Julia made a few notations in her PDA before they motored off. "Seems you've got everyone convinced I *am* a miracle worker."

Trent turned away from the road to look at her. "Too much pressure?"

"I work best under pressure," Julia admitted honestly.

Trent cast her a satisfied nod as if he'd known that about her already. His faith in her was a bit daunting, though she couldn't deny it was also an ego boost.

Next, they drove toward the outer edge of Crimson Canyon, where the blue cloudless sky met with the scarlet packed earth. Trent pulled to a stop facing the seemingly groundless canyon as they stared out. "That's Shadow Ridge. It's my favorite place on the property."

"I can see why." The beauty of nature pulled at her, making her feel small and minute, but inspired and strong at the same time. "It's glorious and untouched."

Trent remained silent for a minute, and then shook his head. "Most guests don't get out that far. It can be dangerous terrain even with a good horse. The Jeep can't get close enough, but trust me, nothing much can match the rock formations and the hues of color at Shadow Ridge."

Julia whipped out her PDA and made a notation. "Okay," she said, her mind spinning at the possibilities. "Where to next?"

Twenty minutes later, after Trent gave her a scenic tour of the rest of the property, they pulled up to Destiny Lake. "We have swimming holes, fishing and non-motorboating here. It's the only natural lake in the vicinity. When I bought the land, I made sure the lake was included."

"A deal breaker otherwise?"

"You got it. I knew I'd build the hotel close to the lake."

"You said there was a legend?"

"There is." Trent got out of the Jeep and walked over to her, opening the door. "Take a walk with me." He put out his hand.

Julia grabbed his hand and once out of the Jeep, she released him. They strolled along the banks quietly as early October breezes blew by. Off in the distance, a few hotel guests splashed in the lake, their laughter a soft whisper on the waters.

Trent took her hand again when they came upon a small boat dock jutting out onto the lake. Three rowboats, tied to the dock, rocked gently in the rippling current. They walked halfway to the end of the dock then stopped to look out at the land.

"This land was settled over one hundred fifty years ago. People who'd tried their luck in the California gold mines and failed, and others who'd never quite made it that far west claimed this area. Legend has it that a young girl named Ella and her secret betrothed had a terrible quarrel here. Her parents had picked a more suitable beau for her. Samuel, the boy she'd pledged to marry, gave her an ultimatum—meet him at the lake at sunset to run off together or she'd never see him again. She didn't want to leave her family, but she knew she couldn't live without the boy she loved. It took her a while to sneak out of the house, but when she got to the lake after midnight, Samuel wasn't there. She searched the land and finally spotted him just as he jumped off the ledge and into Crimson Canyon."

"That's awful, Trent, but somehow I knew you'd say that." All legends seemed to end with tragedy, she thought. She'd taken a course in college on the subject. "So you're saying the lake is haunted?"

Trent grinned. "Not at all. The legend goes that the young girl cried all night by the lake, completely devastated. When the sun rose in the morning, she looked up and found her betrothed, dripping wet from his swim across the lake to get to her. It all happened right on the spot we're standing on now."

"Samuel didn't jump off the cliff?"

"No, he tripped on a rock in the dark and hit his head. She thought she'd seen him throw himself over the cliff. That had been his intention, but they'd both been given a second chance. They never ran off, but stood up to her folks, married here and had five children. They lived on this land until they died some fifty years later."

"So that's why it's called Destiny Lake."

"Ella and Sam didn't name the lake, but their children did, once they'd heard the story."

"The two were destined to be together. They were given a second chance." Julia gazed out at the lake, thinking about the two lovers for a second, the romantic in her taking hold of such an inspiring love story. Then, she took out her PDA again and punched in some key words. "Okay, got it." She turned to Trent. "Will you take me back to the office now? I've got a lot to do today."

Trent didn't hesitate. He guided her back to the Jeep and they drove off, her head filling with ideas to make the miracle Trent wanted come true.

Three hours later, Julia sat at her computer as ideas formulated in her head. Tempest West needed something…more. She knew they'd have to organize a new or grand opening, but she also knew that she needed a different approach. After taking the tour of the grounds, she'd come to the conclusion that an elite western resort with beautiful scenery wasn't enough. She had to appeal to the wealthy masses. Give them something they couldn't get anywhere else. She knew what she wanted to do. And she knew it would be risky. But Trent was a risk-taker and once she had all her ducks in a row, she'd present him with her ideas.

Later that afternoon, Julia buzzed Kimberly on the intercom. "Hi, Kim. Do you have those financial reports I requested from Legal this morning?"

"I just picked up the files. I'll be right in."

Julia leaned back in her chair, looking at the Young Dreams Foundation Web site on the screen. Her father had introduced her to the foundation when his best friend's son had been ill and the charity had granted the child's fondest dream of meeting space shuttle astronauts at Cape Kennedy. After that touching experience Julia had gotten deeply involved working with the foundation whenever time would allow, getting to know some of the children the charity helped and making some good friends along the way. An idea percolated in her head and she put it on hold when Kimberly walked in with an armload of files.

"They may have pulled more files than you need," she said with a smile.

"That's okay. I'll take a quick look at them and give you back what I don't need. I know what I'm looking for. Do you have a minute?"

Kim plunked down in the seat across from her. "I do. Tell me what you need and I'll sort through half the files." Kim handed her a stack while keeping several for herself.

Julia thumbed through a few. "I want to see the names and addresses of all the patrons of the hotel since it opened. How long they stayed. How much they spent. I also want our profit-and-loss statements for all the months we've been operating."

"Okay, that's easy."

Kim put her head down and sifted through the files on her side of Julia's desk, while Julia did the same.

Julia took a good look at a file that seemed out of place. "I guess this one got in here by accident," she muttered. When Kimberly glanced up, she explained, "It's a copy of my contract." Julia shrugged and then noted a mistake—the date of the unsigned contract was incorrect. "Must be a typo," she said. "The date is wrong."

"Legal prides itself on never making mistakes," Kim said jokingly. "They go over every word with a fine-tooth comb before sending it out."

Julia glanced at the date again. It had to be wrong.

Trent hadn't come back to Los Angeles to see her, until one week after the date typed in the contract. He hadn't known anything about her losing the Bridges account until he'd seen her that night.

She'd worked with Tempest's legal department enough to know that they were as efficient and fastidious as Kimberly had stated.

She stared at the unsigned copy of her contract, that early date glaring back at her.

Then she blinked.

"He knew," she said under her breath, trepidation crawling up her spine.

"What?" Kim glanced up again. "Did you say something to me?"

"Uh, no." Julia tossed the files down on her desk, deep in thought, emotions wreaking havoc with all rational thought.

She peered at Kimberly. "You know what, just leave everything here. I'll sort through this stuff by myself and give it back to you when I'm done."

Kim nodded. "Okay. If you're sure."

"I'm sure," she said and stood. Kim rose as well and turned to leave.

"Uh, Kim?"

"Yes?" She turned fully to face her.

"How long have you worked for Tempest? Since the beginning?"

"Yes, I was here when we opened. I transferred from the Tempest in Dallas."

"So you'd know what my office looked like before?"

Kimberly nodded, appearing slightly puzzled and Julia added, "I'm just thinking about a color change."

"Oh, but it's so feminine and pretty now. It seems to suit you. Mr. Alonzo, our first marketing vice president, wanted dark oak, dark walls and dark shutters. It was so dreary, I hated coming in here."

Julia's heart raced. She didn't like the suspicions bouncing around in her mind. "I don't suppose you remember when Trent had the office remodeled?"

"I sure do! It was on my birthday. Mr. Tyler gave me the day off, so I couldn't possibly forget that. It was on a Friday. He had a whole crew come in and redo the office and when I came back on Monday, everything had been changed. That was exactly one month ago tomorrow."

Julia's stomach clenched and she flinched. "One month ago?"

Before Trent had come to her apartment in Los Angeles with flowers and sweet words of apology. Had he known all along about her losing the Bridges account? Or had he… Julia closed her eyes and steadied her trembling body. Had he orchestrated her losing that account somehow?

"Yes, one month." Once again Kim nodded, then looked at her with concern. "Is anything wrong?"

"No, I'm fine." She managed a brief smile. "I'd better let you get back to work."

"Okay." Kimberly walked out of the office and Julia leaned forward, bracing her hands on the edge of her desk.

"It couldn't be," she muttered, while a deep sense of dread coursed through her entire system, telling her it very well could be. She knew about Trent's bet with his brother. She knew about his competitive streak; he'd told her countless stories about besting Brock when they were younger. Making his hotel succeed meant more than money to him. He had something to prove.

Thoughts flashed in her head.

Miracle worker.

I checked you out.

Trent's timely reappearance in her life at about the same time he'd fired his marketing VP and one week after she'd lost the Bridges account seemed too coincidental not to have been premeditated.

She hadn't thought about it before, but now as she glanced around her office, she noted how very well this office suited her. The wall colors and soft carpeting and even similar pieces of artwork on the side table resembled her L.A. apartment, despite the western theme. She might have thought it a nice touch, if Trent had gone to the trouble *after* he'd secured her employment here, rather than *before*.

How deceitful of him. How arrogant.

Her entire body trembled with fury. Before she condemned him to the gallows, she'd confront him. Grabbing the unsigned contract, her only tangible evidence, she strode out of her office. She filled her lungs with fortifying oxygen, yanked on Trent's office doorknob and flung the door open.

"Hold on, Brock," Trent said into the receiver. Covering his hand over the phone, he looked at her. "Give me a minute, darlin'. I'm almost through."

"You're through now," she growled. "Hang up the phone, Trent."

Trent's brows rose in surprise. "What the hell?" He cast her a confounded look then returned to the phone. "I'll call you later." He hung up the phone and stood, gazing at her with annoyance. "What's bothering you?"

"Just answer one question for me, Trent. Did you or did you not orchestrate my losing the Bridges account so I could work for you?"

Trent narrowed his eyes. "What gave you that idea?"

She tossed the unsigned contract onto his desk. He glanced at it, his expression giving nothing away.

"Just answer the question, Trent. Truthfully…if you're capable."

His brows rose and a tic worked at his jaw. "I made a deal with the restaurant chain, yeah."

"And was I part of that deal?"

Trent walked around his desk and then leaned against it, bracing his hands along the edge. "Close the door, Julia."

She turned to slam the door then faced him again, folding her arms across her middle, too furious to move. She stood there, waiting, irked by his nonchalant posture.

"Well?"

"Were you part of the deal?" He took a minute to

answer, his mouth tight, his eyes cold. "Yeah. I wanted you to work for me."

"So you sabotaged me!" She blew up, her fury unrestrained now. "Do you know how hard I worked on that Bridges account? Do you have any idea what landing that account would have meant to me?"

"I'm paying you a very generous salary," Trent said. "Nothing I did was illegal. The people at Bridges wanted this deal with Tempest. They've been pursuing us for years."

"What deal?" she asked, her fury mounting. He hadn't even tried to deny any of it.

"They'll be putting their restaurants in our hotels in strategic cities across the country. We've been in private negotiations for some time now. I simply made that happen sooner than expected. Everyone stands to win."

"Except me!"

"That's a matter of opinion."

"Ha! You lied to me over and over again, Trent! You've nearly destroyed my reputation making me lose that account. I took this job on the rebound. We both know that. Tempest West is one hotel. If you call that winning then I'd rather be a *loser* and sign a contract with an entire restaurant chain."

Trent pushed away from the desk. "Now you have a *binding* contract with me."

Julia's blood boiled. "A binding contract? You tricked me into this. I can't believe you plan to hold me to that contract!"

Trent let go a deep sigh. "It's not the end of the world. I'm a businessman. I saw an opportunity and took it. We'd been leaning toward Bridges anyway. Eventually we would have made the deal with them."

Julia shook her head. "I don't believe you."

"Believe it," he said firmly, his lips thinning. "It's the truth."

"No, the truth is, you're ruthless and coldhearted! You used me to get what you wanted. We had a great time together after your brother's wedding and when you left L.A., I never heard from you again until Tempest West got in trouble. Then out of the blue, you're knocking on my door, bringing me orchid bouquets, wining and dining me, *seducing* me. That's as low as it gets. I'm a bright girl but even I hadn't seen that coming. You're a first-class bastard, Trent Tyler."

Trent flinched and his nostrils flared. "Simmer down, Julia."

"I don't think so. I'm at my boiling point now. You've hurt me, Trent." Not only had he almost destroyed her professional life, he'd wounded her personally. She'd confided in him and he'd used that knowledge to injure her. When would she learn not to get involved with men she worked with? "You're not denying any of it?"

Trent blew out a breath. "No. It was a sound business arrangement."

She tossed her head back and laughed at the absurdity. "And I thought you were different. The cowboy with the slow hands and soft touch is nothing more than a corporate con artist. What a fool I've been!"

He'd damaged her reputation, her ego and her heart. She'd never give him the satisfaction of knowing she'd almost fallen in love with him. She'd never trust him again.

Trent took a few steps her way.

"Stop!" She put up her hand and stood her ground. "Don't, Trent. You're not going to charm your way out of this one."

He halted his approach, his lips tight, his jaw twitching. "You agreed to the terms and signed the contract."

"That's all that you care about, isn't it?" She spit out the words. "Doesn't matter that I signed under false pretenses."

"There's nothing false in that contract. I didn't force you to sign on the dotted line. Your job is to promote and market Tempest West and keep us in the black this year."

Julia lifted her chin. "Yeah, well…I'm not sure I'm willing to do that anymore."

"Darlin', the contract is airtight. You've got no choice." Trent cast her a smile that ordinarily would have her melting in his arms.

"I could fight you on this."

"You'd lose. It would become public knowledge that you abandoned your contract when the chips were down. No one forced you to sign on with Tempest West. My deal with Bridges was legitimate and there isn't one person there who wouldn't agree." He sat at his desk and leaned back in his chair. "Unless you want your reputation ruined, you're staying."

Four

Blackmail. Deception. Seduction.

As the sun set on the horizon, Julia sank into the sofa in her suite and sipped on Merlot, her nerves shot, her body quaking. She thought about Trent and the lengths he'd gone to, to secure her skills for Tempest West.

His lies and manipulations made her feel a fool, but nothing hurt her more than the way she'd succumbed to his charm. She'd been putty in his hands. He'd shown up on her doorstep a few weeks ago and all of her business sense had vanished. She'd been mesmerized and satisfied by a great lover. He'd blinded her to the truth. Maybe if she hadn't been so vulnerable when he'd shown up, she might have figured it all out.

Or at least been suspicious.

But the tall, gorgeous, seemingly earnest Texan had her fooled.

He was right about one thing though. As much as she may want to, she couldn't abandon her position here. She needed a solid account for her resume. She'd lost the Bridges Restaurant deal and had no further prospects at the moment. She'd have to stay and make this work. She wasn't a quitter, no matter the circumstances.

She was professional and she'd signed a contract. Then there was Evan and Laney to think about. They were her friends. She wouldn't want to cause a rift in their friendship by accusing Trent and causing trouble at Tempest West.

Her answer was simple—do her job and steer clear of Trent at all costs. Sabotage flitted across her mind for a second, but Julia wasn't built that way. Once she'd made up her mind to stay on, she'd do nothing but her best. Her career and reputation were on the line, just as much as Trent's.

An hour later, once she could formulate rational thoughts, she picked up her cell phone and auto-dialed Laney's number. They'd known each other since grammar school back in Los Angeles, and nothing cheered her up more than speaking with her best friend.

When Laney answered, Julia calmed just hearing her voice. "Mrs. Tyler? You're the winner of a brand-new bouncing baby boy! Your prize will be awarded in exactly three months."

On the other end, Laney's bright laughter settled Julia's heartbreak a little. "Hi, Julia. I think I'll take my winnings now. Can you manage that?"

"Oh, I wish I could. Having a bad day?"

"Not really. Just the usual. I'm a little tired tonight and Evan's doting on me like a mother hen."

"How nice of him." It was too bad that *nice* trait didn't run in the family.

"Hmm. I suppose," Laney said. "True, my tummy's getting as big as a beach ball, but I'm not an invalid. I read somewhere that it's the first-time father syndrome. I'm not used to Evan, hovering. His eyes bug out when he feels the baby moving in my stomach."

"I wish I was there to see it."

"To see Evan's eyes bugging out, or my stomach growing?" Laney asked.

"Both. I miss you, Laney. I miss L.A."

"Oh, Julia. I thought you were thrilled to be working at Tempest West. And, well, after what you told me about Trent and you, I thought you and he, might have…"

"We have a working relationship, Laney." Julia wasn't ready to tell her friend how she'd been manipulated. She wasn't sure she'd ever tell her. Evan and Trent were close and Laney didn't need any awkwardness in her life right now. She'd just recently recovered from months of morning sickness. She didn't want to dampen her spirits in any way. Julia was resigned to deal with Trent on her own—she'd complete her six-month contract then dash out of town, leaving the hotel and

Trent Tyler in the red Arizona dust. "I do love the challenge of working here. It's…a beautiful location." That much was true, but Trent had ruined her excitement about coming to live here temporarily.

Now, it was just another business arrangement.

There was a slight pause on the opposite end of the phone. Julia hadn't confessed to Laney about her brief whirlwind affair with Trent right after their wedding months ago, but she had confided to her about how Trent had swept her off her feet a few weeks ago, coming to her rescue with this job offer.

Laney had always been perceptive when it came to matters of the heart. "Why don't I believe you?"

"It is beautiful here," she repeated, skirting the real issue. "But we need to get down to business. I'm throwing you a baby shower in six weeks remember? Can you e-mail me your guest list, hon? I've rented out a room at Maggiano's," she fibbed. "And I've arranged to be back in town for the entire weekend."

"Yum, Maggiano's. I'll eat Italian for two! I'll get that list to you today, Julia. This is very sweet of you. I know how busy you are."

"I'm looking forward to it, Laney. I want my future *nephew* to have lots of great gifts when he arrives."

"It's so exciting. I know I've got several more months, but I can't wait."

They ended the conversation on a happy note and Julia poured herself another glass of wine. When a knock sounded at her door, she walked over and opened it.

Trent stood on the threshold, his gaze touching hers.

"Checking on your investment?" she asked, leaning on the doorjamb, sipping Merlot.

"Something like that. You didn't return to work today."

"I took the afternoon off," she said coolly. What could he do, fire her? "Don't worry. I'll be up at the crack of dawn, plugging away to make all your dreams come true."

Holding his impatience at bay, the tall, dark-haired Texan filled the doorway and took a sharp breath. She wished she was immune to him, but with her emotions so tangled, one touch from him could make her crumble. At the moment she hated him, vowing she'd never let him get close enough to touch her ever again.

"Maybe I was worried about you," he said.

"Maybe snow will fall on the Arizona desert."

He let go an aggravated sigh. That tic worked his jawline again. "You know," he began, "it doesn't have to be this way."

"Oh, I think it does," Julia said, refusing to give him an inch. "In fact, it's the only way it can be between us now." Trent deserved every bit of her disdain.

"Okay, fine, Julia. Be in my office first thing in the morning. We have plans to discuss."

He turned and walked away before she could slam the door in his face.

Tomorrow, she'd have to discuss Laney's surprise baby shower with him. They'd have to work side by side, fixing the problems at Tempest West.

But tonight, she could simply fall into bed and forget she'd ever met Trent Tyler.

Trent hadn't met a woman he'd wanted more than Julia Lowell—any other female would surely pale in comparison. She sat across his desk with her head down, diligently laying out her plans to improve the status of Tempest West. He noted the dark curling lashes touching her eyelids, a soft full mouth grazed with cherry lip gloss and a slender kissable throat. Her long hair caressed her shoulders and touched the scooped-out neckline of her red business suit.

She wore that color like no other, and those sandals…? She'd worn them deliberately to torment him.

She hadn't walked into his office this morning with a sourpuss, feeling sorry for herself. She'd come in holding her chin high, her eyes filled with determination. She'd kicked herself into business mode, giving Trent time to admire her gumption and her beauty.

"These are my preliminary plans. What do you think of them?" she asked, point-blank, and making eye contact.

Trent nodded. "I think you've got a handle of what needs changing around here."

"Tempest West is special. It's not just a resort—those are a dime a dozen. We need to give our clientele an unforgettable experience. Something they can't get anywhere else. It's going to be exclusive, by invitation only, in the beginning. That's a risk, Trent. Are you willing to take it?"

Julia had smarts. Trent recognized that in her, even as he'd covered his body over hers and made her moan his name the first time they'd been together. Yet, she could very well be setting his hotel up to fail.

He'd put all of his trust in her when she'd first arrived. But now that she knew the truth about his hiring her, would she still give him one-hundred-percent loyalty and dedication?

He narrowed his eyes. "Is this the same plan you'd been working up before our conversation yesterday?"

Julia took no offense at his question. She straightened in her seat and cast him a thin-lipped smile. "We had great sex, Trent. You used me professionally. I'm furious with you, but I'd never compromise my principles. I believe in fair work ethics. So, if you're asking if I'd throw you to the dogs out of spite? The answer is no. This is the same plan I had formulating in my head since I arrived here."

"I had to ask."

"Granted. Now, what do you think about my ideas?"

Trent scrubbed his jaw, the day-old stubble grating against his fingers. His mind shifted to a few days ago, when Julia had straddled his lap, shaving him with smooth careful strokes until he couldn't take it another second. He'd tossed her onto the bathroom counter, wrapped her legs around his waist and drove his body deep into her soft folds, the shave long forgotten.

He let go a sigh. "I'm willing to take the risk. It's a great idea."

This time Julia smiled wide, her eyes bright. "I'll get working on the new marketing slogan for the hotel. We need something catchy that will go hand in hand with the theme of Tempest West. It's going to take some thinking."

"Let me know what you need from me."

Julia glanced at his mouth. A flicker. A quick look that had Trent wondering how long she'd stay angry with him and deny them both those long, hot, sexy nights in bed.

"I work best alone, Trent. When I have something, I'll bring it to you for your approval."

He nodded, his eyes dipping down to the collar that sat low on her chest, teasing him with a hint of cleavage.

"Fair enough."

They stared at each other for a long moment.

Then Julia commented, "You're not going to apologize for what you did to me, are you?"

He might, if he thought she'd land in his bed tonight. "No."

She nodded with resignation, only the slightest tremble of her lips giving away her contempt. "We need to talk about Laney and Evan's baby shower. Laney thinks I'm giving it in six weeks."

Trent looked at his appointment book. "I've got appointments the rest of the day. Meet me for dinner tonight and we'll discuss it."

She shook her head. "I can't. Fit me in sometime else."

"You can't or *won't?*" he asked.

"Won't." Her delicate chin lifted. "Besides, I have plans for the evening."

Trent slammed his appointment book closed.

"I'm not available to you after working hours." She smiled. "Keep that in mind from now on."

Trent got her message loud and clear. There was a funny thing about claims like that. Once issued, Trent would do everything in his power to change the fact.

She gathered up her papers and set them in a manila folder then rose. She was halfway to the door when she turned "Tell me, Trent? Is there a sign painted on me somewhere that says, 'Take advantage of me'?"

Trent rose and walked around his desk, holding her gaze. "All I see is a gorgeous, sexy woman with brains and talent, darlin'."

Julia put her head down before meeting his eyes again. "I'm afraid it's too late for charm, Trent."

She walked out of his office, leaving him to wonder what kind of plans she had tonight.

And with whom?

Julia sat atop a sturdy bay mare that Pete assured her was the gentlest horse in their string. He rode beside her as they made their way out of the stables heading west to the far edge of Crimson Canyon.

"There are some places so beautiful out here that the paying guests never get a chance to see," he said.

"That's what Tre—uh, Mr. Tyler told me. Why do you suppose that is?" Julia asked. Saddle leather squeaked and stretched as Julia adjusted her rear end in her seat.

Pete shrugged. "It's remote. Some areas are more dangerous than others. When we take them on a guided tour, we stay on certain tried-and-true paths for safety's sake."

"That doesn't sound like Trent Tyler. He wants everyone who comes here to experience the land."

"It wasn't his idea. We had an incident here when the hotel just opened." Pete shook his head. "Some folk think they've got riding skills they don't. One man thought he could climb up a ways on Shadow Ridge. He wanted a bird's-eye view of the canyon. He pushed his horse and made it partway up, when a big old red-winged hawk swooped down and spooked his mount. The guest was thrown from his horse. His pride was injured more than anything, yet he blamed the management for not putting up warning signs. He threatened to sue for our neglect. Mr. Tyler calmed him down and talked him out of suing. Since then, we give guided tours only and stick to these paths."

"What a shame," Julia said, looking in awe at Shadow Ridge, the steep awe-inspiring crest of Crimson Canyon.

"Prettiest land you'd ever want to see."

"It must be something because I can't imagine anything more beautiful than what I'm seeing out there now."

"Take my word on it."

"I'd like to see it." Julia smiled at Pete. "Take me there."

Pete looked at her. "The sun's about to set, Miss Lowell."

"It's Julia and I know. That's the plan. I want to see it just before sunset."

Pete nodded and nudged his gelding into a slow trot. Julia's mare followed.

More than an hour later, Julia returned with Pete from the ridge of the canyon. They dismounted in front of the stables and she handed him the reins. "Thanks, Pete. I enjoyed the ride. You've enlightened me with your knowledge of the area."

Pete grinned. "It's been a while since I've enlightened anyone, about anything, Miss Low—" he said, then caught himself. He'd called her Miss Lowell five times after she thought she'd convinced him to drop the formality. "Julia," he said, finally.

Both laughed, thoroughly enjoying the moment until Trent walked out of the stable, his expression grim. He eyed Pete for a second, and then shifted his gaze to her.

Pete seemed undeterred by Trent's presence, yet Julia's nerves rattled and her smile faded. "Evening, Mr. Tyler," Pete said, tipping his hat.

"Pete." He headed straight toward them, his gaze now fastened on Julia. Only then did she notice his Jeep outside by the office. "Is this why you couldn't have a dinner meeting with me?"

Julia wanted to roll her eyes, but she managed to keep them steady on Trent's face. "Yes," she admitted, revealing the truth. She'd arranged to have Pete take her up to Shadow Ridge this evening. Clearly, by the look Trent gave her, then Pete, he wasn't happy with either of them. "I told you I had plans this evening."

"We were just going inside to have us a drink after

our ride," Pete said, handing off the reins of both horses to one of the wranglers. He looked Trent in the eye. "Care to join us?"

Julia admired Pete's nonchalance with his boss. He was a man who didn't mince words or play deceptive games. She liked Pete and wondered if he knew that Kimberly had a serious thing for him.

"No, don't think I will. I need to speak with Julia. I'll take her back and make sure she gets a drink."

Julia bristled. She wasn't one to cause a scene, but this was the second time in so many days that Trent had tried her patience.

Pete looked to Julia. "If you need that drink, I'll run inside and get it for you."

Julia was tempted. She'd rather not give in to Trent's demands. Even though Pete held his own she didn't want to cause trouble between the two men.

"That's okay, Pete. It's getting late. I'll ride back with Mr. Tyler."

Trent turned on his heel and sauntered back to his Jeep. Julia did a mental count to ten, and then smiled at Pete. "Thanks for going out of your way for me tonight. I really did enjoy the ride."

"Anytime." He tipped his hat. "The boss is waitin'," he said with a grin. "You don't want to get on his bad side, being a new *employee* and all."

Julia's eyes widened. Pete saw too much with those clear blue eyes. "You're not afraid of him, are you?"

"Of Trent? Hell, no. He knows I'm a damn good

wrangler and I keep my nose clean. And I know he's a fair employer and a decent man. We got mutual respect."

He grinned again.

"Julia?" Trent called from the Jeep.

Mutual respect. She wished she had gotten her job the conventional way, by coming in for an interview and dazzling Trent with her ideas, rather than having him use deception to gain her employment. Then maybe they'd share mutual respect and she'd think of Trent as a decent man. As it stood now, she had nothing but contempt for him.

She thanked Pete again then climbed into the passenger side of the Jeep and slammed the door, facing straight ahead. As Trent drove off, he turned to her. "You don't waste any time."

She wouldn't allow Trent to goad her into an argument, but his comment did manage to irk her. "I don't. Not when I have a job to do."

"You're saying that sunset ride had something to do with work?"

"It had everything to do with work." She rested her head back on the seat and closed her eyes. "Were you following me?"

"No, Julia. I wasn't following you. I came out tonight to check on my own horses."

She opened her eyes and turned to face him. "You have horses here?"

He nodded. "Two. Duke and Honey Girl. I come out to see them whenever I can. Ride them if I have time."

"So what was so urgent that you needed to pull me away from my conversation with Pete?"

He wished he knew. He'd come out of the stables fully prepared to return to his office when he spotted Julia and Pete, looking as if they were enjoying each other's company a little bit too much. "If you need time with me, it'll have to be tonight. I'm leaving town in the morning. Have some meetings I've put off too long as it is."

"How long will you be gone?"

"A few days."

"Okay," she said on a sigh.

Trent drove to his house on the property and pulled the Jeep into his personal garage. He pushed the remote and the door lowered behind them. Beside the Jeep sat his black Chevy Silverado and his silver-toned BMW.

"Where are we?" she asked, puzzled.

"My house," he said on a shrug.

Julia's eyes widened. "I thought you lived at the hotel."

"I do, mostly. But I had this house built for those times when I need to be alone. It's small and basic and has a pretty glorious view of the canyon."

"Why'd you bring me here?" she asked pointedly. Julia looked like a caged animal ready to break through the bars.

"You need the names and phone numbers for the Tyler family, right? I keep my personal files here. Come on, Julia. I'm not the big bad wolf. You'll get what you need and have a drink then I'll take you back to the hotel."

He got out of the Jeep and waited for her. Once she relented, he took her arm and guided her inside.

Trent had this house custom-built to suit his needs. With one huge master bedroom, a spacious kitchen and eating area and a great room that housed a large suede sofa facing the ceiling-to-floor stone fireplace, Trent wished he'd had more time to spend here. "This is it."

Julia's pinched expression softened. She glanced around, seeing all of the rooms except the bedroom from where she stood. "It's nice, Trent. I can see why'd you like to come here to unwind."

He'd love to do some unwinding with her right now. He'd never brought a woman to this house before and the fact that he'd done so without thinking made him glad he was leaving Tempest West for a few days.

The image of Julia laughing with Pete by the stables made him balk. Having sex with Julia was one thing, getting emotionally attached was another thing all together.

"Have a seat," he said and gestured to a corner on the L-shaped sofa. "What'll you have to drink—wine, champagne, something mixed?"

He walked over to the built-in bar next to the fireplace. "Just ice water, please."

Trent looked at her and laughed. "You really do think I'm the big bad wolf, don't you?"

"Let's just say, your hood is off now. I know who I'm dealing with."

"Ouch." Trent looked at Julia sitting on the sofa,

dressed in soft denim jeans, her legs crossed, her posture stiff. Even in leather boots and casual clothes, she looked elegant and classy and sweetly beautiful. Long dark wisps of hair had blown across her face from the Jeep ride and tendrils caressed her cheeks. Trent poured her a glass of ice water, and a tumbler with whiskey two fingers high for himself, then walked over to hand her the drink.

He sat down beside her. "Pete's got a reputation with the ladies," he said, sipping his whiskey.

"And you'd thought to warn me?" She looked at the glass she held. "That's rich, Trent, considering what you've done to me."

He leaned forward, bracing his arms on his legs, and turned to her. "You're not letting this go, are you?"

She shook her head, speaking softly but with conviction. "No, I'm not. And I'm not interested in Pete. My only interest at Tempest West is to do what I came here to do, then move on."

Delicately, she sipped from her glass and Trent cast his gaze to her mouth. A drop of water remained on her lip. She licked it dry absently.

He lifted his gaze to hers and her expression faltered for a brief second, her pretty green eyes going soft before she set her chin rigidly. There was still chemistry between them, sizzling like steam in a hot shower.

"When would be a convenient time for Laney's baby shower?" she asked, changing the conversation to business again.

"Whenever it suits you. I'll have the company jet

ready to pick up your guests. We'll put them up for a night or two. Give them access to all the facilities."

"I'd like to do it in a few weeks, before Laney gets suspicious. I'll have to let Evan in on the plans to get Laney here. I thought, since it's partly true, we'll use the excuse that you're having an open house for the family."

Trent nodded. "Sounds like that would work. I'll play along. Anything else, darlin'?"

"Just those names and numbers please. I should be getting back now."

They finalized plans and Trent drove Julia back to the hotel. He parked the Jeep and turned to her. "I'll be back on Friday. Kimberly knows how to reach me, if you need anything."

"I won't."

"You've made that clear, Julia. But I was speaking about business, darlin'."

"Right." She swallowed and nodded. "By the time you return, I'll have finalized my new marketing strategy."

"I'm looking forward to it."

He got out of the Jeep and walked around to open her door. She slipped out easily and he walked her inside the lobby to the elevator.

"I'll see you on Fri—"

Trent leaned in and kissed her before she could finish her thought. He brushed his body to hers, holding her firmly on the waist, and parted her lips, driving inside to taste her again. "Needed that," he whispered, stroking her hips up and down gently with the palms of his hands.

"Don't," she breathed out, a futile attempt to deny them both what they craved. "Trent, I'm never going to forgive you."

"I know, but you're not a fool, darlin'. Me and you, we're great together." Her slight tremble and the surrender of her body in that one moment would sustain him for the next few days. "And you'd only be lying to yourself if you thought you didn't *need* that kiss the way I did."

Five

Two days later, Julia tried to think of anything but Trent.

When she wasn't head-deep in her work, she'd think of her last encounter with Trent, his hot lusty kiss and the lingering look in his eyes. Whenever he touched her, every nerve in her body came alive. She wished it wasn't so. She'd never reacted to a man the way she did to Trent.

He had it all—good looks, charm, undeniable sex appeal, intelligence and that darn Texas swagger that turned her body to Jell-O whenever she spotted him walking her way. Sometimes, especially when he worked his wiles on her, or kissed her unexpectedly, she forgot that he was as ruthless as he was handsome and as unyielding as he was charming.

She'd found a measure of relief in his leaving town for a few days. But she also hated to admit that she looked forward to seeing him when he returned.

Which was absolutely crazy.

He'd manipulated her and lied to her. Seduced her and made her feel a fool. Her head told her to forget he walked the earth, but her heart…that was another matter.

Well past the dinner hour, Julia sat at her desk, staring at her workup of the new ad campaign until her eyes blurred. She'd had an artist rendering of Crimson Canyon sketched on a poster and had struggled with the exact wording for the campaign. The image for Tempest West facing her, she felt the immediate pull and knew she was on the right track.

She sipped stale cold coffee and grimaced. "Awful," she muttered, setting the cup down. She sat back in her chair and sighed, deciding she'd taxed her brain enough these past few days. Her stomach growled, reminding her of the late hour.

She rose and stretched her arms. Loosening her taut muscles, she closed her eyes and moved her head slowly, making tension-relieving circles.

"You look sexy when you do that." Trent stood at her office threshold, leaning on the doorjamb, hands in the back pockets of his jeans.

"You're back," she stated, stunned to see him. Not only had he surprised her, but she also didn't like the sudden heart surge he evoked.

His eyes flashed and he smiled. "Miss me?" He strolled into her office.

Like a rat invasion, she thought, but kept her comment to herself. "I was just leaving for the night."

He ignored her and focused on the poster on her desk. "Is that it?" he asked, walking over to take a better look.

Julia hesitated. She liked her ideas and thought she'd nailed down the campaign, but she hadn't yet prepared her presentation. She liked to have all of her ducks in a row, especially when it came to her profession. Yet, Trent always seemed to knock down a duck or two in her well-ordered life.

"Yes, that's it. But I'm not through yet. I still plan on designing a special invitation for our grand reopening. Only I doubt we'll call it that."

Trent kept his gaze on the poster. "Live our legends," he said, reciting the words, "or create one of your own."

She moved to stand beside him. "Right there," she said, pointing to the bottom band of the poster, "we'll put the words *Tempest West at Crimson Canyon.*"

Trent slanted her a look. "I like the slogan."

"Thank you," she said softly. Then amid the silence of the room, her stomach grumbled again.

Trent grinned. "I'm starving, too. Came straight here from the airport. The chef is sending up dinner. Enough for two."

Julia nodded. "I'm sure you can eat it all," she said, opening the drawer and reaching for her purse.

"Glazed salmon rubbed with herbs over rice pilaf."

It sounded like food heaven. She shook her head.

"Carrot soufflé."

"Soufflé?" she questioned, her mouth watering. "Doesn't sound like a cowboy's meal."

"My appetite knows no boundaries."

She smiled weakly.

"Chef's sending up seven-layer chocolate cake, too."

"The house specialty," she muttered.

"You can fill me in on the details of the campaign," he said, "while we're having the meal."

Another soft rumble from her stomach made her shuffle her feet uneasily but if Trent heard, he made no mention of it. She'd planned on ordering a salad from the Canyon Café and getting to bed early tonight.

A gourmet meal sounded a thousand times better.

She just didn't have enough willpower to refuse both the meal and Trent. "Is this an order from the boss?"

Trent looked deep into her eyes. "No, just a request."

She let go a sharp sigh, denying that his earnest reply meant anything to her. "Okay, then. When do we eat?"

Trent glanced at his watch. "Should be up in a few minutes."

Julia made herself busy, clearing her desk, setting the poster aside and filing away paperwork. Trent walked over to the window and looked out, apparently deep in thought. "I just made a deal to have a herd of wild mustangs brought to the canyon."

"What?" Julia thought she heard wrong.

Trent turned from the window to face her. "They need a good home, Julia. They're beat up and battered and hungry."

"Trent, this isn't a ranch. It's an elite resort hotel—one that has a long way to go to make a profit. Why didn't you discuss this with me before?"

He shrugged and shook his head. "My mind was made up. We'll make it work, Julia. I'm setting them loose behind Shadow Ridge."

"Loose?" Julia's mind spun. "Tell me your kidding."

"The herd won't bother anyone out there. It's unofficially off-limits to our guests."

"If you'd waited for my presentation, you'd know I had very specific plans for Shadow Ridge. And those plans do not include wild horses."

His jaw was set firm and his eyes showed his determination. There'd be no talking him out of this, she feared.

"What kind of plans?" he asked.

"Private guided tours up to the ridge on horseback. Art lectures. Given by professionals. The privacy, the peace and quiet and the gorgeous vistas of Crimson Canyon—I don't know too many people who wouldn't love finding a secluded area so breathtaking you can't believe it's real, to reflect. Some would paint or sketch. Some would ride. We'd be offering them something they can't get anywhere else, remember?"

"Now they'll have open-range views of wild horses," Trent said.

"Can you contain them?"

"I won't," he said adamantly.

Julia had to admire his dedication and the compassion he had for the neglected animals. She envisioned those horses, well cared for and free to run. She knew Trent would see to their welfare. He was a man who took care of his own.

"But the safety of the guests—"

"The herd will have natural boundaries, Julia. They won't stray too far. I plan on feeding them and making sure they have water. They'll stay where we need them to stay. And they won't bother anyone."

"How can you promise that?"

"Trust me."

She'd never place her trust in him again. But it was his hotel and his money to lose. "You can't afford a lawsuit."

Trent raised his brows. "You heard about that?"

"Not from you. But, yes, I did hear about it. Our first priority is to your paying guests, Trent. And they'll be paying almost double for what I'm proposing. Please tell me you don't have anything crazy planned for Destiny Lake? No Jet Ski stunt shows or anything?"

Trent's mouth twisted. "Cute, Julia."

"Well?"

"No. I don't have plans for Destiny Lake."

"That's a relief," she said.

The waiter strolled by her office pushing a rolling cart. When Trent spotted him, he gestured for him to come inside. "It's dinner for two now, Robert," he said. "We'll eat right here at the desk, unless Miss Lowell would like to eat downstairs?" Trent glanced at her, apparently looking for a change of heart.

"This is fine. We're working," she said, offering a small smile to Robert.

The waiter glanced at the meal. "I'll be back with another plate and set of utensils."

Robert was halfway out the door before Trent stopped him. "Don't bother, Robert. There are enough utensils here for both of us. Thanks for bringing it up." Trent saw him to the door and handed him a tip, then returned to uncover the plates.

Steam rose up and rich, savory flavors blended in the air, causing noises to erupt in Julia's stomach. "Looks delicious."

Trent took all the dishes from the cart and placed them on the desk, then sat down.

"Now what," she said, hungering for the meal. Trent had dismissed Robert and there were no extra plates.

"Now you can either sit beside me," Trent said, his voice soft and low, "or sit on my lap and I'll feed you myself. Sounds like a great way to enjoy a meal."

A sensual image flashed in her head. She strolled to where he sat and bent down to face him, coming very close to his face. Looking in his gorgeous dark eyes, Julia resisted the temptation. "I'll be right back," she said.

"Where are you going?" he asked.

"You'll see."

A minute later, she returned from the lounge behind the receptionist's area with a paper plate and plastic utensils.

Trent only smiled. "Resourceful."

"I think so," she said and Trent slid her the fine china and cutlery, then filled a paper plate of food for himself and waited for her to sit before digging in with his plastic fork.

If nothing else, Trent Tyler had manners.

The next morning, Trent parked the Jeep by the stables and walked inside the office. It irked him again, seeing Julia conversing with Pete, her soft laughter filling the small room as she kept her focus trained on the head wrangler.

He trusted Julia about as far as he could toss her so he'd insisted on taking her up to Shadow Ridge and having her spell out her plans, step-by-step. It was the only way to fully envision her concepts.

What she proposed was risky and Trent didn't mind taking a calculated risk when necessary, but he had to make sure Julia wasn't trying to screw him over to gain revenge.

He wasn't sure she was capable of such deception, yet he hadn't expected her to be so darn hard to win over again. He wanted her back in his bed, plain and simple. And he wanted to believe in her new marketing strategy—the latter being extremely important.

"Mornin'," he said, interrupting their conversation.

Julia looked up with a smile on her face. "Good morning."

Pete nodded a greeting and excused himself, leaving them alone in the office.

"You ready for a ride?"

"Yes, I even dressed for the part," she said, her good mood overflowing. Trent would have engaged her, except he knew Pete had been the one responsible for her cheery attitude.

Dressed in jeans and a soft cotton blouse, her hair pulled back in a ponytail, her face free of makeup and looking as fresh as a sunny day, Trent couldn't deny her natural beauty. Whether elegantly dressed or in a business suit or looking like a rodeo queen, Julia Lowell made an impression.

"Let's get going."

"Are we *burning daylight*," she teased.

Trent roped an arm around her waist and brought her up against him. Her delicately soft body made him hard as granite.

"Oh," she breathed out.

"Something's burning, darlin'. And if we don't get out of here soon, you're gonna find out what that is."

Tension crackled between them. They stared at each other for a time, before he released her and she mumbled, "Okay, I-let's go."

Trent cursed under his breath. There wasn't a woman he wanted more, but he'd damned well wasn't about to let Julia befuddle him into making a big mistake.

Trent strode out the door and walked over to the corral housing his horses. Pete had Duke and Honey

Girl saddled up and ready. Trent grabbed the reins. "Thanks, Pete. I'll take it from here."

Pete glanced at Julia, who was steps behind. "Gotcha," he said with a nod. "I'll be back in the office if you need me later. Have a good ride."

Trent helped Julia mount the mare then climbed onto his own horse and they rode off. As they made their way to Shadow Ridge, he let Julia do most of the talking, laying out her plan. He listened intently and nodded, taking in the view of saguaro cactus dotting the property and the inspiring flame-colored mountains of Crimson Canyon. While they rode, his frustration cooled as he concentrated on Julia's vision.

"What made you think of offering art lectures?" he asked.

"Not your everyday art lecture, Trent. We'll employ a real artist at Tempest West. He'll show his work in the hotel gallery and then we'll offer inspiration at the most picturesque place on the property. When I checked your previous clientele questionnaire I noticed the majority of guests were lovers of art and music. Sounds like a no-brainer to me to entice guests with what they love. Remember, Tempest West isn't an overnight stay on the way to a destination. It *is* the destination. And we need to give our guests what they love. Give them no reason to leave for outside entertainment. The word *exclusive* will be synonymous with Tempest West. That's our selling point. Privacy, seclusion, natural settings and exclusive opportunities."

Trent reined in Duke when they reached the base of Shadow Ridge. "Sounds good."

Julia's mare followed Duke's lead and stopped beside him. "The artist will come to show his work and become better known in the art community. Your clientele are very wealthy, Trent. They'll spend extra money for what we offer. As for the singer, I've worked with Sarah Rose with the Dream Foundation Charity."

"You got us Sarah Rose?" Trent was impressed. Country singer Sarah Rose was as famous and talented as Reba McEntire and Faith Hill.

"I did. I'm working out details with her management. But I've spoken with her privately and she's ready for a change of pace. She needs a vacation. Once I described Tempest West, she was willing to come and do a few intimate shows weekly as long as we guarantee her privacy while she's here. She'll be a guest as well."

Trent looked deep into Julia's pretty eyes. Her passion for her work came though loud and clear. She seemed convinced and that was good enough for him. "If you say it'll work, I'm all for it."

"There's never any guarantees, but I think so. It's all in the packaging, Trent. I'm working hard on a special invitation with the new slogan and I'm having a new brochure made up."

"Okay," he said, then glanced at the ridge looming above. "You ready to make this climb?"

Julia peered at the ridge shadowed by morning light. "Pete says there's another way up."

"It's a longer winding path. But, yes, there's another way up."

"Show me."

Trent led Julia to the top of Shadow Ridge using a well-hidden path that wound back and around the mountain. He dismounted once they reached the plateau and helped her down, holding her close as she slid down his body from Honey Girl.

Her eyes flickered as she stared at his mouth.

Trent smiled and moved away, taking her hand in his. "Is this your vision?" he asked, walking to the center of the elevated flatland that looked upon Crimson Canyon, where naturally sculpted rock formations met western skies.

"Yes," she breathed out. "This is it."

"I see it, too." Trent wrapped his arm around her waist and they stared out at the amazing vista.

Quiet. Secluded. Natural.

Julia's voice broke the silence. "If you could find a way to broaden the path up here, I don't think the guests would mind the longer ride on horseback. It's the safest way up and they'd be well-guided."

"I'd planned on setting the mustangs loose behind the ridge."

"Can't you set them in the canyon?"

"No, they'd starve. They wouldn't be any better off than where they were rescued from in the first place. We wouldn't have a way to care for them down there."

"This is important to you, isn't it?"

"It is," Trent admitted, enjoying the feel of Julia's body sidled up close to his. He'd been too long without her and no other woman would do. "I can't sit by and watch those horses die." Trent owned a massive amount of land. There was room for the hotel *and* the herd. Though he'd grown up with his brothers in a midsize town, Trent had dreamed one day of owning enough land to maintain a wild herd. He'd always had an affinity for horses and when he'd found out these mustangs were dying, he'd had to help.

Julia's voice softened. "Is it more important than the success of the hotel? You could lose your bet with your brother."

"Darlin', that's not going to happen. I always find a way to get what I want."

Julia set her hand on his cheek, her caress the lightest feather touch, her eyes filled with regret. "Yeah, Trent. I know."

Six

Baby shower guests arrived by company jet one day before the surprise party. Kimberly helped Julia greet them at the airport and usher them into Tempest West limousines to get the group to the hotel by midmorning.

With Trent's assistance, Julia had arranged for a barbecue welcome lunch on the outside patio facing Crimson Canyon and a guided ride up to Shadow Ridge this afternoon.

Tomorrow, she'd hold the surprise baby shower on the banks of Destiny Lake. In a sense, it was a trial run for her new vision for Tempest West. Her baby shower guests would be privy to the hotel's exclusive five-star treatment she'd planned for paying guests later in the month. It was a special treat for her, because her father, being a dear friend of Laney's, was also an invited guest. She hadn't seen him in weeks and she gladly welcomed his presence. They'd hugged and kissed at the airport and Julia was glad he'd made the trip.

There was no equal to a father's love.

And right about now, Julia needed the support. She'd been dodging Trent's advances since he'd manipulated her so expertly. He'd made it clear that he wanted her. Julia's resistance had waned some, allowing him a kiss or two in the past few weeks. At night when her mind wandered she'd dream of being in his arms and allowing him free reign over her body...and laying claim over his. Keeping the sexy cowboy a safe distance away was easier said than done.

An hour later, Julia spotted her father standing next to Trent and a lovely gray-haired woman under the lattice covering on the patio. She walked across the inlaid stone path and was immediately introduced to Rebecca Tyler, Trent's mother. "This is my Julia," Matthew Lowell said, smiling at Rebecca.

Rebecca lent her hand and Julia took it. "It's very nice to finally meet you, Mrs. Tyler. And for such a happy occasion."

"Oh, just call me Rebecca, please," she replied with a sweet smile. "I'm thrilled that I'm finally going to be a grandmother. How nice of you to have this surprise for Laney."

"She's my best friend. I'm happy to do it."

"I've been hoping for the same, Rebecca," her father said, "but Julia's career-minded at the moment. No babies on the horizon for me."

"Dad!" Heat crawled up her throat. She stole a glance at Trent, who'd been watching her intently.

"I've been lobbying for years, Matthew," Rebecca said.

Trent nodded. "Can't deny that. Mom's put the word out loud and clear. She could show Washington a thing or two."

"Is that what it takes?" her father asked, smiling at Rebecca.

"It's been quite a while," Rebecca started, "but seems to me it takes a bit *more* than that."

Her father let out a chuckle.

Julia lifted her brows. Her father was flirting with Rebecca Tyler and the pretty woman flirted back.

Rebecca glanced at Julia. "My son thinks you have brilliant ideas. He's shared some of them with me and I have to say I'm glad you're here working together, dear. Trent doesn't give praise lightly."

"Thank you, Rebecca. I'm doing my best for—" she hesitated and peered at Trent "—for Tempest West."

Trent brushed shoulders with her. She caught the musky scent of his cologne and the firm stance of his body next to hers. "Julia's going to change the image at Tempest West. Fact is, I'm banking on all her ideas. I trust her completely."

Julia's breath caught hearing those words. Trent had never failed to believe in her abilities. She'd never given him reason not to, but hearing him say it to his mother and her father softened her heart.

"Thank you," she said, refusing to look at Trent. "I'd better check on the other guests. It's almost time for lunch. Rebecca, it was very nice to meet you. If you'll both excuse me now."

"You go on, honey," her father said. "I'll make sure Rebecca finds a seat."

Trent kissed his mother on the cheek. "I'd better get back to work, Mother." Then he turned to her father. "Nice to meet you, Matthew." Trent shook her father's hand. "You both enjoy your lunch. I'll see you later."

Julia headed for the lobby and before she got halfway there, Trent placed a hand to her back and steered her away. "I need to talk to you," he said, guiding her toward the cottages on the property. "It's important."

The walk toward the cottages reminded her of that late-night tryst they'd had when she'd first arrived at Tempest West. "It's business, right?"

"Right," Trent said, keeping her moving and refusing to glance her way.

Once they'd reached the farthest empty cottage, Trent maneuvered her into a lushly landscaped secluded terrace. "I'm not going inside with you, Trent." Memories flashed of torrid bodies and steamy sex.

Trent released his hold on her waist and walked to the far end of the walled terrace. She watched as he paced back and forth. "Did you tell your father how you came to be hired here at Tempest West?"

His question struck home and she knew why he'd been adamant about privacy. "You mean how you seduced and tricked me?"

"That's your take on it. Did you tell him?"

Julia made him stew on her answer a little while. She sighed and took a moment, meeting his direct gaze.

"Well?" he asked impatiently.

"No, Trent. I didn't tell him. But not out of any concern for you. I didn't tell him, because one, I didn't want him to know I'd been so easily fooled. I do have some pride. And two, because he'd probably insist on me leaving Tempest West immediately. He has an unrivaled work ethic, not to mention a protective streak for his only daughter."

"Darlin', you don't need protection from me." He took a step toward her.

Julia raised her brows. "Don't I, Trent?"

"No. Hell, we make a damn good team. In and out of bed."

Julia ignored his comment because deep down she knew it was true. Other than his initial sabotage, they'd worked together pretty darn well these past few weeks. He was competent, efficient and easy to approach with new ideas. As for *in* bed, Julia was certain she'd never find a better sexual partner. "Why are you so concerned about my father knowing the truth?"

"You saw them together, Julia. Your father and my mother. Damn, I can't believe I'm saying this, but there were sparks between them. You must have noticed."

"Couldn't miss the fireworks," Julia said. "Ironic, isn't it?"

Trent moved closer and lowered his voice to a rasp. "Why? Because a Lowell finds a Tyler attractive?"

Julia shook her head. "Because it's *my* father and *your* mother, Trent."

That's all Julia needed. She'd hoped she'd read too much into their brief conversation just minutes ago, but Trent, too, had noticed. Her father had been extremely lonely lately. From what she gathered, so had Rebecca Tyler. She'd lost her husband years ago and had never remarried.

Good heaven, she didn't need any more ties to Trent. But she'd never seen her father so smitten before. Her father seemed truly interested in Rebecca Tyler.

Trent approached her, coming closer yet, his gaze darkened and his presence creating hot tremors inside. She backed up against the wall. "Trent, go away."

He placed his hands on the wall beside her head. Trapped, Julia could only stare into his hungry gaze. "Make me," he said, brushing a finger along her jaw.

His touch erupted goose bumps. And her tremors intensified, racking her body. Rational thought escaped her and her heart pounded with longing. She breathed in his scent, the earthy familiar remnants of his cologne turning her inside out. "What…do…you…want?"

"Fireworks." He bent his head and swept her up in a kiss that would have knocked her down if he hadn't slid his hands to her waist. He pulled her close and held her steady.

Julia craved him. He was a thirst she had to quench. The tall, rugged Texan could always push her buttons and make her squirm with desire.

His kiss stole her breath. She wrapped her arms around his neck, bringing him closer. He groaned when their bodies locked, his erection undeniable.

He slanted his mouth over hers again and deepened the kiss. Julia savored every second of it, forgetting all the reasons she should push him away.

Trent Tyler wasn't a man easy to dismiss.

"Meet me tonight," he said, between kisses. "Spend the night at my place."

His place? His small cozy home set on the outskirts of the property. Oh, how she wanted to. In a perfect world where Trent could be trusted, she'd meet him in a heartbeat and they'd spend a glorious night together. Julia had a healthy sexual appetite and Trent had spoiled her in that regard. He'd treated her to every female fantasy she'd ever entertained and she'd begun to feel more for him than any other man who'd come into her life.

But Trent was far from *perfect*. He'd turned her well-ordered world topsy-turvy.

"You know I can't," she said breathlessly. "My father's here." The reminder of her father's presence worked better than a cold splash of water.

He broke off the kiss and stared at her.

"And so is your mother," she said, taking the opportunity to duck away the minute he released his hold on her. She kept three feet between them. "They'll expect to spend time with us tonight."

Trent acknowledged her with a slow nod. "Guess I forgot about that." His gaze traveled to her mouth, which was tender from his passionate kisses. "I invited my mother to dinner."

"And I invited my father," she said, straightening up her red-and-white polka-dot summer dress.

Trent glanced down to her sandaled feet and arched a brow. "Those shoes were gonna be part of our fireworks display."

Julia swallowed and peered at her cherry-red sandals.

He brushed past her, then stopped, swung his arm around her waist again—bringing her up close—and kissed her quickly. "Next time, darlin'."

He took off, exiting the secluded terrace with a bone-melting swagger, removing all doubt as to why she had a weak spot for such a hardheaded cowboy.

Julia sat beside her father at dinner, facing Trent and his mother outside on a terraced balcony with Destiny Lake in the distance. Moonlight glistened on the still glasslike waters, the silence of the night only interrupted by the quiet whispers of other diners on the terrace. Thick candle pillars flickered, setting the handsome Tylers across the table in soft shadows.

When her father announced that he'd invited her boss and his mother to dinner, Julia hadn't shown her displeasure and hid her mental fit of frustration. The thought kept niggling at her that Rebecca Tyler could become an important person in her father's life.

It spelled disaster.

As soon as her job was finished here, she wanted nothing to do with Trent Tyler ever again. She'd have a hard time getting him out of her head, but he'd proven over and over again that he couldn't be trusted. She wasn't competing with another woman, but rather his drive to succeed with Tempest West at all costs.

"I'm very proud of Trent," Rebecca said, after the wine had been poured. "Tempest West was his vision and he wouldn't let anyone discourage him from his dream."

Her father raised his glass. "Let's toast to Tempest West and our kids, Rebecca. Seems we both have children with vision."

"Why, yes. That's a wonderful thing to toast, Matthew."

Amusement evident in Trent's eyes, Julia squirmed in her chair. Toasting to Trent's vision was equal to rubbing salt in her wounds.

She was the last to raise her glass, but with her father's watchful gaze on her, she submitted and four glasses clinked together. Julia looked away and took a big gulp of her Merlot.

As much as she hated to admit it, she'd enjoyed the rest of the meal. Trent made easy conversation with her father about sports while she and Rebecca had a lovely talk about fashion and art and raising her boys in a small town.

"The Texas just washed out of my other two boys,

but Trent clung on to his roots," Rebecca said. "Evan and Brock adapted to city living easily, but not Trent."

Rebecca glanced lovingly at her youngest son.

"Now, Ma," Trent teased, swaying his head Jethro Bodine style. "Don't you go on about me, like that."

Rebecca put her hand over Trent's and squeezed. He cast his mother a sweet look and smiled.

The moment wasn't lost on Julia. She witnessed the love and warmth between them.

When her father suggested they all take a walk along the lake after coffee, Julia was the first to decline. "Oh, Father, I'd love to, but I need to get to bed early tonight."

She'd gone up to Shadow Ridge with the willing guests this afternoon and the ride went according to plan. She'd come back extremely pleased that her trial run had worked out and everyone seemed in awe of the views up there.

"That's okay, honey. You've got yourself a big day tomorrow with the baby shower."

"I can't wait to see Laney," Julia confessed. "I'm hoping the surprise goes off as planned."

"It will, sweetheart," her father said. "You're always on top of your game. I'm sure she doesn't suspect a thing."

"I hope so, Dad."

Matthew faced the Tylers at the table. "Trent? Rebecca? Are either of you up for a walk by the lake?"

Rebecca nodded readily. "That sounds lovely."

Trent sent a look Julia's way, contemplating. "No, thanks. I've got to catch up on some work. I want everything set, so I can spend time with Evan and Brock tomorrow."

"My three boys rarely see each other now that they're living in different parts of the country," Rebecca explained.

When they finished the meal, Trent rose and helped his mother from her chair, his manners during dinner impeccable. Julia rose when the others did and she bid them a good-night, thanking Rebecca for her suggestions and advice about Native American and western art.

Julia watched her father walk off with Trent's mother, her heart in her throat. If it had been any other sweet-natured woman, she would be thrilled. Her father deserved some happiness in his life again.

"They're a good match," Trent said, watching the two head toward the lake. Then he turned to Julia. "You must hate that."

Appalled at his blunt assessment, though it was partly true, Julia snapped, "Your mother is very sweet. Nothing like you."

The jibe bounced right off him. "Admit it, darlin'. You can't stand the implications—my mother and your father together."

"*Together?* My mind won't go there."

"It might have to. Your father is actively pursuing my mother. And my mom's not complaining one bit."

"For heaven's sake. They only just met!"

"The way we'd only just met...at my brother's wedding?" Trent raised one brow provocatively.

Julia squeezed her eyes shut briefly. "Now that's an image I don't want in my head."

"It may be that Tylers are attracted to Lowells. Could be genetic. But I'm thinking it's more a matter of excellent taste."

Julia's heart dipped. She stared into Trent's gorgeous dark eyes. The corners of his mouth lifted up in a heart-warming smile.

"You've got an open invite to my home, Julia. I want you there...with me. Anytime, day or night." Trent left her and walked toward the back entrance to the lobby.

Knees weak, Julia lowered herself down in the chair, holding on to the side arms for dear life. If only Trent meant it for real. But in her heart she knew that he would discard her the minute her contract was up. Once she helped Tempest West thrive, once Trent won that bet with his brother, he'd move on.

She'd been victim to his charm once before and she'd been deeply injured. All he truly cared about was his hotel.

"Julia, are you okay?" Kimberly appeared in front of her.

"Kim? You're still here? I thought you'd be exhausted after the ride up Shadow Ridge today."

"I am tired." She plunked down in the seat next to her at the table as busboys cleared the dishes. "But I stayed late to finish up some office work."

Julia smiled. "You're dedicated."

"And a bit frustrated."

Julia forgot about her problems with Trent to focus on Kimberly. "What's wrong?"

Kim shrugged. "It's Pete. I finally got up the nerve to speak to him. We've seen each other on the grounds three times and we've talked. I've been as obvious as I know how to be without jumping his bones and I *think* he's interested, but then…nothing. He tips his hat, smiles and walks away."

Julia stared down at the tablecloth. She was the last person anybody should ask for dating advice. What was she thinking trying to hook Kim up with Pete? It was a classic no-brainer. Don't get involved with someone you work with. "Sometimes, its for the best," she mumbled.

"What? Is this the same woman who orchestrated leaving me alone with Pete the other day?"

"That wasn't planned," Julia explained, having a change of heart. If what Trent said about Pete was true, Kimberly could get hurt. "I had good intentions, but some things aren't meant to be."

Kim narrowed her eyes. "You're not talking about Pete anymore, are you? I've seen the looks you and the boss give each other. You two have Fourth of July sparks."

"Sometimes sparks blow up in your face, Kim. I've had an office romance before. It didn't work out and it was awkward for a long time afterward."

Kim stared at Julia. She lowered her voice. "I'm sorry."

Julia shrugged. "Ancient history."

Then Kimberly confided, "I think I'm in love with Pete."

Julia laid a hand on her arm softly in full understanding. Matters of the heart should be treated delicately. "I think maybe you might be. Let things develop naturally. Be patient and see where it goes. Forcing it would be a mistake."

"I'm trying to be patient. It's hard."

Julia nodded. She hadn't been too smart with Trent, yet she'd tried to rectify that lately. "Sorry. I haven't been very encouraging tonight."

"I get it, Julia. You're in love, too."

Julia's eyes widened and she lifted her brows in surprise. "No. I'm not."

The words fell easily from her lips, but somehow she doubted Kimberly bought her denial.

"Okay."

"Let's forget about men for tonight and focus on the baby shower," Julia said. "I'm so grateful that you're helping me tomorrow."

As the women rose and laced arms, walking off together, Julia's mind filled with cherub-faced sweet-smelling babies and powder-blue frosted cake.

Much happier thoughts.

It was an old-fashioned baby shower the way Julia and Laney had always planned while sitting together in their Queen of the Island chairs at the beachfront café back in Los Angeles when they were young girls dreaming their grown-up dreams.

Julia had a massive white tent set up by the lake, only a stone's throw from the dock. Tables for eight covered with blue-and-white tablecloths were decorated with flower arrangements, little glass baby bottles filled with candy and teeny hand-knitted baby bootie favors.

She had games set on the tables, ready to go, and if the men in the group groaned, Julia wouldn't care. They'd play the toilet paper wraparound to guess Laney's belly size and do baby crossword puzzles.

An ice sculpture shaped like a baby holding a bottle in a bassinet sweated a bit in the Arizona morning heat, but Julia had been assured that it had three full hours of ice-life, before dripping into a puddle.

The invited guests were in their seats, and with the flaps to three sides of the great tent down they were hidden from view to anyone walking out of the hotel's back entrance. All was ready and Julia waited impatiently now, anxious to pull off the surprise and see her friends.

Brock Tyler, Trent's brother, sidled up next to her. "Trent said they've arrived and settled into their room. He's bringing them outside now for a tour of the grounds."

"Thank you," she said, staring into the same deep, dark Tyler eyes. Brock was handsome, but not in a rugged, no-nonsense way like Trent. With his hands thrust in the pockets of his pleated black slacks, wearing custom-tailored Armani, Brock had a devil-may-care look about him.

A heartbreaker of a different kind, she presumed.

"Sure glad Evan's having the first Tyler grandchild," he said with a grin. "Takes the pressure off."

"Your mother is thrilled."

"Enough to lay off me and Trent for a while?"

Julia shrugged. "I don't know her that well, but I suppose she'll want more grandchildren…eventually."

"That'd be Trent's job next."

Julia snapped her head up, envisioning Trent as a father.

Brock stared at her, caught her contemplating, and winked with a knowing nod. "I thought so."

"What?" she asked, his cocksure expression claiming that he already knew too much about her relationship with his brother.

He leaned over and whispered in her ear, "If my brother's *not* dating you, I'd worry about him."

"Oh, we're not dat—"

"Here they come," Kim called out, waving her cell phone. "I've got spies who said they just exited the hotel."

Brock ushered her inside the tent and she checked the flaps again, making sure they were secure. "Please, everyone, stay as quiet as you can. Trent will bring them around to the open end of the tent."

Just minutes later, Trent led Evan and Laney to the front side of the tent facing Destiny Lake.

"Surprise!" everyone called out.

Laney took a step back, her eyes widening and her expression filled with astonishment. She scanned over the tables, at all of her closest friends and family standing now with smiles, clapping and applauding. Her gaze connected with Julia's and tears filled her eyes. "Oh, Jules, this is just how we…"

She couldn't get the words out and Julia rushed over to her. They embraced, Julia hugging as tightly as she could with Laney's growing belly separating them. Then Julia grasped her hands and stood back to survey her friend. "You look beautiful, honey."

Evan kissed Laney's cheek. "That's what I keep telling her."

He kissed Julia on the cheek next. "You pulled it off. Laney didn't have a clue."

"I didn't," she said to Julia in awe. "Thank you, Jules. This is…perfect."

Laney turned to her husband. "You knew all the time and kept this from me? You're good, Evan. Really good."

Evan agreed with a nod. "I keep telling you that."

Then the guest of honor focused her attention on the guests. Surrounded by friends, close work associates and relatives, she wagged her finger at all of them. "You guys didn't let on." She narrowed her eyes playfully. "I don't know if I'm going to trust any of you ever again."

They all laughed.

Evan took Laney's hand and they entered the crowd, hugging and greeting everyone. Julia's father and Rebecca Tyler approached the pregnant couple together. Another notch of dread seeped into Julia's system for a second, but her joy at seeing Laney so happy pushed her momentary hesitation away.

Trent issued an order to pull the flaps of the tent aside, and three men worked to secure them so that all views of the lake and grounds were visible now. Warm, fresh morning breezes lifted away the heat and Julia couldn't have asked for a more glorious day.

"You did it," Trent said with a hint of admiration.

Julia relaxed for a moment and sighed with pleasure. "I wanted everything just right. I'm pretty happy with the results."

"Miracle worker in action," Trent teased.

Julia smiled and with a tilt of her head, she bantered back, "Say that now, but we'll see how much you like me when I have you diaper an infant doll."

Trent's expression paled and Julia laughed. "All the men at the shower will have to compete, I'm afraid. And you, *Uncle Trent,* will go first."

Julia turned away from Trent, showing Evan and Laney to their seats at the main table, and announced that brunch would be served.

The waiters appeared with the first course and Julia made sure everyone was tended to, making the rounds and speaking with the guests until she felt a strong hand gently grab her arm from behind, guiding her to the main table.

"Sit," Brock ordered with a charming smile as he ushered her into a seat next to Laney. Brock took the seat on the other side of Julia. She faced Trent across the table, but he wasn't looking at her.

Eyes narrowed to slits, Trent glared at his brother and

the arm he'd placed possessively along the back of Julia's chair.

Laney chuckled low enough for only Julia to hear. She leaned over and whispered, "Tylers are very competitive when they want something, honey."

So she'd gathered, and Laney, her dear perceptive friend, hadn't missed a thing. Apparently pregnancy didn't dull a woman's intuition, but rather fine-tuned it to maximum accuracy.

Julia wasn't any man's prize. She picked up her fork and dived into her cucumber salad, ignoring the handsome man beside her and the gorgeous cowboy who'd destroyed her trust in men sitting across from her.

Seven

"I can't forgive him, Laney. I don't trust him one bit," Julia said that night. Within minutes of being alone with Laney, Julia had spilled the beans about her relationship with Trent, leaving out nothing. Laney wouldn't have it any other way and they had the perfect opportunity to talk since the Tyler men were having drinks outside at the Sunset Bar.

She lay across Laney's bed in her suite after helping her make a thank-you list for the gifts she'd received today. Julia tied and untied the ribbon on a particularly pretty two-inch-wide blue bow she'd taken off a package sitting on the floor.

Laney closed the baby book she'd been looking over

while sitting in a comfortable leather wing chair and met her gaze. "Trent's very ambitious. And competitive. But he's worth fighting for, Julia."

"So you think I should forget what he's done to me?"

"Evan set out to destroy my father's company and I forgave him."

"No offense, honey. But you didn't have much choice."

Laney patted her stomach lovingly. "You mean because I got pregnant?"

Julia nodded, hoping she hadn't been too blunt.

"It was the best thing that could've ever happened to me. If not for the baby, Evan and I might never have gotten together. I really did hate him," she said. Then her face split into a wide grin. "For about a second."

"My situation with Trent is very different." Julia yanked at the bow and untied it for the last time, letting the ribbon flow in folds onto the floor. She sat up on the bed and crossed her legs. "My pride took a beating. Trent hurt me."

"But he wants you, Julia. I only had to see him with you today for a minute to notice that. Brock should have burst into flames from the looks Trent sent him." Laney giggled.

Julia smiled, the image fresh in her mind. "I noticed that." She found it a small consolation. Trent competed with Brock it seemed, in every way. "How come Evan isn't part of this huge competition between Brock and Trent?"

"Because he's madly in love and doesn't play those games anymore," Laney said in all seriousness. Then she burst out laughing. "I'm joking, Evan is highly competitive, too. But his father died when the boys were young and since Evan was the oldest, he took on a lot of the responsibility. Besides, Evan wants the hotels to thrive and isn't above a good healthy competition between his brothers. Everyone stands to gain."

Julia understood that, she just wished she hadn't been the pawn in Trent's game.

Laney set the baby book aside and leaned forward, taking Julia's hand. "Hey, I've never seen you like this. He's really gotten to you, hasn't he?"

Julia answered honestly. "From the minute I laid eyes on him. How can I allow myself to fall for a man I can't trust? I should have learned my lesson with Jerry Baker. He was a social climber and used me to further his career. The two men are hardly different, in my eyes."

Laney rose from her chair and took the space beside Julia on the bed. Shoulder to shoulder, they sat quietly for a time then Laney broke the silence. "If Trent hadn't done what he did, you wouldn't be here right now."

Julia nodded. "I'd be on the career path I'd chosen for myself."

"Would you give up everything you've done here? The experiences you've had, if you could go back?"

"You mean, if I'd never gotten involved with Trent?"

Laney looked her in the eyes. "Yes. Would you trade not knowing Trent at all, for what you gave up? Think about it."

Julia thought about Trent. Rugged and handsome, intelligent and fun—when they were getting along she'd thought Trent was everything she wanted in a man. She'd envisioned a life with him. What woman wouldn't want their own personal five-star cowboy? "Not a fair question, Laney."

"Maybe it's not a fair question, but sometimes we have to take that leap of faith," Laney said. "We have to go out on a limb to get what we want. Even when we're not granted any guarantees. What Trent did to you was awful. He made a mistake—"

"He doesn't think so," she interrupted.

"Okay, so he's not perfect, but I happen to know he's a good man in a lot of ways. His biggest flaw is that he's blinded by ambition. Evan was like that, too. The right woman can change that in a man."

Julia listened to her friend, taking it all in. Still puzzled, she asked, "Are you saying I should dive in headfirst without knowing if there's enough water to sustain me?"

Laney laced their hands and applied slight pressure. "Only you know how to answer that question." Then she smiled. "You and I will always be like sisters. But wouldn't it be great if we were both part of the same family? I'd love nothing more."

The pleasing thought spun around and around in her head, but still, Julia couldn't bring herself to believe that would ever happen. "You're still dreaming our Queen of the Island dreams, Laney. I think I might have outgrown them."

"Don't you even think it!" Laney's expression fierce, she declared, "You're going to get everything you want in life, Jules. Even if I have to knock some sense into Trent myself."

Julia grinned at Laney's keen protective nature and she loved her all the more for it. "I appreciate the thought, but you promised not to say a word. I'm holding you to that promise."

"Yeah, well, maybe I shouldn't have promised." Laney stood to stretch out her back. She arched and extended her form, her belly protruding a little farther out.

While Laney would disagree, Julia knew those happily-ever-after dreams weren't meant for everyone on the planet, but she wouldn't argue the point with her pregnant best friend.

"Oh!" Laney said, her expression one of awe and delight as she reached for Julia's hand. She laid it atop her rounded belly and Julia felt the wave of movement and then a sharp little aggressive kick.

"Say hello to your aunt Julia, baby," Laney whispered.

"Hello, baby Tyler," Julia said softly, thrilled for her best friend and anxious to meet the new life coming into the world soon.

She refused to allow thoughts of her own problems mar this one precious sweet moment. Tomorrow, Laney and Evan and all the guests would go home. Things at Tempest West would go back to normal.

Julia would focus on work and try to keep from falling in love with Trent Tyler.

* * *

"You like her," Brock said, nudging Trent's shoulder as the three Tyler men unwound at the bar.

Trent turned from the bar and leaned against it to look straight out, staring into the darkened landscape illuminated by thousands of sparkling stars. October breezes with just the right bite of cool ruffled him more than Brock ever could. He sipped his whiskey, the dark hard liquor sliding down his throat easily. "Guess again."

"You're definitely hot for her," Brock said.

Trent didn't have to look at Brock to know his mouth curled into a cocky grin.

He shrugged. He'd had years of practice not allowing Brock to best him. "None of your business."

Ten tall tables edged with inset stone and tan rawhide stools surrounded the small area designed as a quiet respite for the Tempest guests. Manned by one expert bartender, Trent had always enjoyed this outdoor bar made with indigenous stone to look as though it had been carved right out of Crimson Canyon.

"She's gorgeous," Brock said. "I'd guess she's got brains, too, since you hired her to pull this place out of the Dumpster. I got to know her a little today."

"You flirted and she didn't flirt back," Evan said, with a grin. "Now *that's* a smart woman."

Nonplussed, Brock went on, "Is that a challenge, big brother? You know I love a good competition."

Evan put his palms up in a stopping gesture. "That's

between you and Trent. I'm just stating the obvious. Your charm took a nosedive today."

Trent let out a chuckle.

Brock took exception to his laughter. "If you're not interested, I want her numb—"

"Back off." Trent set his highball glass down and looked Brock square in the eye.

His brother turned away with a quirk of his lips, nodding. "I guess I got my answer." He took the last shot of his drink then gestured to the bartender for another Jägermeister. "There's a rumor going around about how quickly our Bridges Restaurant deal went through. Seems it has something to do with you hiring Julia."

"She tell you that?" Curious, Trent wondered how much Brock knew about Julia's involvement at Tempest West.

"Let's just say, I've got good instincts," Brock said, with a split-second smile. "And I can put two and two together. We'd been stalling on that for months, and suddenly, you're pushing for Bridges Restaurants, making it happen."

Trent shook his head. "You're sure doing a lot of contemplating for a guy who thinks he's going to win. Maybe you're running scared after seeing this place?"

"Running scared? Hell, no. I'm going to beat you hands down. This place," he began, darting a glance around, "isn't half-bad. It's got atmosphere and style. But it's remote and doesn't offer enough to keep the patrons coming back."

Trent took exception to that. He believed in Julia's ideas for Tempest West. "If you're so sure, want to up the ante?"

"You mean aside from putting our egos and pride on the line? What did you have in mind?"

While Trent thought about a suitable prize, Evan interjected, "How about the *bird?*"

"Right, that's yours, Ev," Brock said, his voice edged with envy. That classic Thunderbird had been sitting in his mother's garage for years and recently she announced that she was ready to part with it. In fact, she insisted. "By rights, that car goes to you."

"Since you're the oldest son," Trent enjoyed pointing out.

Evan twitched his lips. "Ah, but I've got everything I want now. And I'm not a car buff. I never wanted it half as much as you and Trent did. Both of you would look at that car with drool dripping from your mouths when you were kids. I'd planned on giving it to one of you anyway, just couldn't figure out which one. This is better than drawing straws, isn't it?" he asked. "Since both of you are sure you're going to win the bet."

Trent and Brock looked at each other and nodded. It sounded like a good plan. Evan was right, Trent loved the car and dangling that carrot would only add to his determination to make Tempest West a success. "I'm game."

"Me, too," Brock said.

Trent shook his brother's hand. "Deal?"

"Deal."

* * *

"Since you both stood up for us at our wedding and since we love you dearly," Laney began, looking first at Julia and then to Trent, "Evan and I would like to ask both of you a question."

Seated beside her husband, Laney grasped his hand as the four sat at the granite-and-oak patio table on their suite's balcony. Morning light cast a glossy smooth shine on Destiny Lake as the sun rose above Crimson Canyon. The table was set with elegant white china and baby yellow roses adorned the center. The scent of freshly brewed coffee filled the air, and the pregnant couple's eagerness only added to the mystery of Evan's invitation to breakfast this morning.

You both have to come for breakfast together.

Laney looked to Evan and when he nodded for her to continue, she smiled and they shared a secret loving look.

A shot of warmth dipped inside Julia's stomach. Oh, to have a man look at her that way. With love and sincerity clearly written on his face. Julia wouldn't hold her breath, but a powerful force inside her said that she deserved to be loved that way. She wouldn't settle for anything less.

Sadly, she didn't think Trent capable of such love, at least not with her. He'd made his priorities clear, so she wouldn't dare to even hope.

Laney's sincere voice broke that line of thought. "Evan and I would be honored if you both agreed to be godparents to our son, when he arrives."

The request took Julia by surprise. She'd always

hoped to have the honor, but hearing Laney say the words made it all so real. Moved to tears, she couldn't get the words out. Overwhelmed by emotion, she could only bob her head up and down.

Under the table, Trent laid the flat of his hand on her thigh. They locked gazes for an instant, the hint of a smile emerging on his face. "I think that means yes. From both of us." Trent gave a little squeeze of assurance then removed his hand from her leg.

Everyone stood and began speaking at once. Evan shook Trent's hand and they embraced, ending with a manly back slap, while Laney and Julia hugged tight as tears flowed freely. The men switched places, Evan thanking her with a kiss while Trent hugged Laney.

Evan poured champagne and toasted to the first Tyler baby's new godparents. "To my brother, Trent," he said.

Laney lifted her flute and added, "And to my best friend, Julia."

Trent and Julia lifted their flutes as well and they touched glass and then sipped champagne. Laney took a tiny sip and lowered her glass first.

"Thank you both. We know you'll make wonderful godparents. I only wish we could stay longer, but I have a doctor's appointment tomorrow."

"And I have to get back to work. Gonna have to pay for college tuition for my son," Evan said with a wink.

Laney shook her head and smiled at Evan's teasing. "Let's get him into Toddler Time Preschool first, before we pack him off to college."

When breakfast ended, they said their farewells with Evan promising to call the minute Laney went into labor. Julia planned on being there for the birth, no matter what. They saw them off, an ivory limo picking her friends up to take them to the airport. Later that day, Julia also bid farewell to the other guests who'd come for the baby shower.

Saying goodbye to her father wasn't easy, especially since he looked a bit forlorn. She'd overheard him telling Rebecca Tyler that he would call her and Julia didn't think he meant that in a platonic way. He'd planned on continuing the relationship and Trent's mother had appeared extremely pleased.

"Knock 'em dead," her father had said to Julia before leaving.

"Of course," she'd answered. "Is there any other way?" And they'd kissed and promised to call each other every day.

Late in the afternoon, Julia leaned back in her office chair, completely lost in thought. There was still so much to do. The invitations were slated to go out this week along with innovative brochures. Tempest West's fresh new image would emerge shortly, hopefully to great fanfare.

She didn't notice Trent enter until she looked up and saw him looming over her desk wearing worn jeans that hugged his lean hips. His black felt hat sat lowered on his forehead, and he wore a dark blue checkered shirt unbuttoned at the throat…and a daring look in his eyes. Her heart tripped over itself.

As a defense mechanism, she went straight into business mode, lifting the mock-up of the invitation. "We're calling it our six-month anniversary party—by special invitation only. A grand reopening gives the impression that something was wrong with the initial grand opening."

"Good thinking," Trent said. He came to the edge of her desk and leaned against it, stretching out in front of her and crossing his legs at the ankles until leather squeaked when his boots touched. He folded his arms across his chest and faced her.

Either the air-conditioning faltered or Julia was having a hot flash because her body temperature ignited like dry brush catching fire. Every time she thought she had a manageable handle on her attraction for Trent, she'd backslide. "Quit looking at me," she snapped, turning her attention to the new brochure layout, but not before she caught Trent's grin—that hot-damn-I've-gotten-to-her cocky smile that made her want to smile along with him.

"I want to do more than look at you, darlin'."

Julia shook her head. "*That's* not going to happen."

"Wanna place a wager on that?"

Julia tossed aside the papers, giving in. Trent didn't want to talk business. A deep sigh escaped when she responded, "There's enough wagering going on around here. I understand your father's classic restored car is up for grabs now."

Laney had filled her in. Trent's father died young, but he'd had a penchant for old cars. He could only afford to restore one, and that was a turquoise-blue 1959 Thunderbird. Laney said it had been his father's pride and joy and all the boys had wanted ownership at one point in their lives.

"I'll be grabbing that prize, sure enough."

His confidence knew no bounds and the trait wasn't something she usually admired. But with Trent, it fit him like a rawhide glove. "I hope you do. It'll mean I've done my job. Now, if you don't mind, I'd better get back to work."

"I do mind," Trent said matter-of-factly. Then he leaned over, cupped her head with one hand and brought her up close. He searched her eyes an instant before kissing her senseless. The kiss lasted for a full minute and when Julia came up for air, she realized that he'd caught her in a weakened moment. Her emotions rocked all over the place from the joys of the baby shower and being asked to be godparent to Laney's son, to apprehension and worry as she watched her father become involved with Trent's mother. She found it exhausting trying to keep her distance from her employer and she had the added pressure of working a miracle at Tempest West. Simply put, Trent knew when she was most vulnerable. He knew what buttons turned her to On. He also knew how to charm the pants off her.

He lifted her to a standing position and she went into

his arms freely, the palms of his hands flat on her derriere, pressing her close enough to feel his solid erection. He said into her ear with fierce quiet, "I want to lay you across this desk and drive my body so deep and long into you that we both forget what planet we're on."

What planet was she on?

Julia glanced at the desk with a deep ache of desire in the pit of her stomach. Trent cocked his head and cast her a quick smile.

"Julia, I had a question…" Kim barged into her office balancing a stack of files in her arms. She came to an immediate halt halfway into the room, a pin-striped frozen statue with wide surprised blue eyes. "Oh, sorry, Julia…*really* sorry," she gushed and backed out of the office as Julia stepped away from Trent. "I'll come back later," Kim muttered, averting her gaze.

"Do that, Kim," Trent said lightly.

Scalding heat raced up Julia's throat. Once Kim vanished, she shook her head and pointed her finger at Trent. "How do you expect me to get my work done if you come in here and, and…"

He shrugged and straightened his frame. "It wasn't planned, Julia."

She balled her hands and set them on her hips. "Wasn't it?"

"There's a reason I came in here." Trent held his cool, but she read beyond his demeanor to see mounting frustration. "And it wasn't to seduce you, darlin'…not that it's a bad idea. If Kim's timing hadn't been so lousy, you'd be naked and spread across that desk right now and we'd be…"

"Enough!" Julia waved away the hot, sexy image but couldn't do much about the tingling between her thighs.

Cocky, confident Trent was back. He grinned. "You like the idea."

Julia's steady rhythm faltered. Trent threw her off balance with his declarations and innuendos. Her well-planned discipline lagged when he smiled her way. Her body betrayed her when he touched her. She peered at the layouts on her desk, hiding the longing he'd uncovered in her. "I have work to do." She blew out another sigh. "Tell me what it is you claim you came in here to say."

Trent cocked his mouth and his eyes danced. "The mustangs are here."

Julia blinked. The wild horses he planned on setting loose beyond Shadow Ridge had arrived.

"I've thought about what you said about endangering the guests. I think I've come up with a solution."

"And?"

"I'd like you to see what I had in mind for them."

His gaze steady, Trent waited for her reply with patience. Julia didn't know which Trent Tyler was more dangerous, the one who would've sent her to cowboy heaven on her desk minutes ago or the one who'd valued her opinion enough to put his ego, money and pride on the line.

"Well?" he asked.

"Let's go," she said, deciding the safer move would be to ride out to Shadow Ridge with Trent rather than be alone with him by her...*desk*.

Eight

"Sarah Rose is here," Kim announced breathlessly, her expression one of awe. "I can't believe it, Julia! I'm such a fan. I love her music."

Julia rose immediately. She'd asked Kim to alert her the minute Sarah's limousine pulled up. "No gushing fans, Kim. Remember, she's coming ahead of time for a little rest and relaxation. We're to treat her as a special guest. Her privacy is essential right now."

"I know," Kim said, wringing out her hands. "I'll maintain, I promise."

"Where's Trent?" she asked, as she strode out her office door, Kim just steps behind.

"He rode out to check on the mustangs again. He'll be back by noon."

All had worked out with the mustangs. Thankfully, Trent had agreed to a compromise and had protected the area up by Shadow Ridge for the guests by putting up a short distance fence and using natural barriers to assure their safety. He'd blocked out a small area of land to do so, thus ensuring the mustangs freedom and affording the guests a good and safe view from Shadow Ridge.

Trent had come through with a viable compromise and Julia had been impressed with the results, admitting that when given all the facts, her employer could be a reasonable man.

Aside from some hot, hungry looks and a few suggestive comments these past few weeks, Trent had been easy to work with and had put their past relationship on the back burner for the time being. Julia was grateful for the reprieve. They'd put their heads together and done a good job of transforming Tempest West into the vision Julia had for the hotel. They'd hired an artist, Ken Yellowhawk—a Cherokee Indian—and arranged for his gorgeous landscapes to be spotlighted in the Tempest gallery. He'd come with a full resume of accomplishments and would spend months here at Tempest, giving lectures, lessons and inspiration to art lovers.

Sarah Rose would draw country-music lovers. The dramatic southwest canyons and sunsets were a perfect setting for her sentimental ballads and lighthearted tunes.

"Okay, that's good," she said to Kim. "Trent will meet her later. I'll show Sarah to her suite and make sure she's settled in and comfortable."

Kim cast her a resigned look, her lips pulling down in a pout.

Julia laughed lightly. "I promise I'll introduce you soon. I need you to check on that added security Trent arranged for Sarah's stay here."

Kim nodded. "He's due in today. Cody Landon."

"He's coming personally? Wow, Trent is really on top of his game." Cody "Code" Landon owned a multimillion-dollar high-tech security agency. From what Trent had said, he was the best in his field and his corporation had ties to the Tempest hotel chains, their security systems being placed in all of their hotels.

"Trent said he insisted on coming personally. Maybe he's a fan, too," Kim added.

"Please let me know when he arrives. I'd better get going."

A thrill coursed through Julia as she rode down the elevator and across the lobby to greet Sarah outside personally. Her vision for Tempest West would soon become reality. No longer deemed as a stopover hotel on the way to something more grand, Tempest West would become an exclusive destination, a place for guests to kick back, enjoy the lakefront views, ride along the canyons on horseback and be privy to private concerts and art lectures given by renowned artists in their field.

Julia had scheduled barbecues around the fire pits called "Hot Roasts" for guests who needed a late-night snack. She'd coerced Pete to give morning tack-and-grooming lessons at the stables before the guests took a ride. Everything was set up to make guests feel like active participants. They could partake in everything planned or simply do nothing at all.

Live our legends or create one of your own.

Julia drew oxygen into her lungs and smiled, feeling that zip of elation when all things came together as planned. On the business front, Julia knew success and felt down deep in her bones that Trent's hotel would thrive. That's all she could concern herself with at the moment.

A chauffeur helped Sarah out of the limousine and Julia waved, walking over to her. "Sarah, hello again. It's so nice to see you."

Sarah straightened and smiled, her green eyes, two shades darker than Julia's and with a hint of aqua, lighting up briefly. "Hi, Julia. It's good to see you again, too. I'm looking forward to," she began with a deep sigh, taking in the surroundings, "just being here."

"And catching up on some well-deserved rest? I promise we won't work you too hard. It's a casual setting. No cameras, no crazy fans. The best part is that we don't have to deal with any arrangements until later in the week."

"Sounds doggone heavenly," she said, her Texas twang coming through.

The auburn-haired woman with curls cascading past her shoulders looked tired and pale. Her pretty eyes faded from their rich hue quickly and Julia sensed that Sarah had come here because she'd desperately needed a rest. Julia didn't read tabloids, but it was common knowledge that Sarah Rose had a daunting day in, day out schedule of concerts, appearances and charity events. Sarah's name had been linked with pro football players, rock stars and movie producers. Julia didn't envy her fame, but rather felt that Sarah had been whisked into an overwhelmingly unfamiliar world from her late teen years.

When Kirby walked up, Julia introduced him to Sarah and noted the appreciation in his eyes. Kirby was a huge country-western fan and Sarah Rose was as famous as they came. He simply tipped his hat politely and gathered up her luggage. Julia made a mental note to invite the aging cowboy to a performance. She gave him the number of the private suite and he and the chauffeur headed in that direction, Sarah's belongings in tow.

Julia wrapped her arm around Sarah's shoulder as they walked toward the entrance of the hotel. "Thank you for coming," she said in earnest. "You're saving my life."

"It just about might be the other way around," Sarah said with a slight forced chuckle. "I need to be here as much as you need me here. I know that's not very savvy to say," she added. "My manager would not approve, but it's the God's honest truth."

From what Julia had gathered from her friendship with Sarah, her manager was a taskmaster and held tight rein on her career. "Well, then, it's a fair deal. I know you'll love it here. And you won't be bothered. Trent's hired extra security to make sure your privacy won't be intruded upon."

"I appreciate it."

"Trent's checking on the wild mustangs, but he wants to meet you."

Sarah stopped when they entered the landing that overlooked the enormous lobby, her mouth dropping in awe. She gazed at the massive floor-to-ceiling panoramic windows to view the landscape. "All this and wild mustangs on the grounds?" Sarah's eyes sparked with delight. "I was raised on a small parcel of land outside of Dallas. It was a ranching community—nothing like this, but it's kinda strange how this place reminds me of home."

"It's serene here, Sarah, and I think you'll have a wonderful experience staying with…" Julia was about to say "with us." But Tempest West wasn't hers. This was Trent's vision and Julia only worked here. She had to remind herself of that time and again when she became too proprietary. "Staying here at Tempest West," she finished awkwardly.

Sarah didn't seem to notice her discomfort and once they arrived at the cottage suite with a wonderful view of Destiny Lake, Julia spent the next ten minutes making sure she felt settled. Julia gave Sarah her private number and they agreed to meet up later in the day after Sarah had a chance to rest a little.

"Quite honestly, I didn't expect you'd come personally," Trent said, shaking Code Landon's hand. He'd found the security expert waiting inside his office after Kim informed him of his arrival just minutes earlier.

"You said you wanted the best."

Trent tossed his hat onto the leather sofa and offered the man a seat. Code sat across the desk from Trent. "I guess I got it." He gave him a quick grin.

Cody Landon was Brock's friend from Texas and recently Tempest hired the Landon Security Agency to oversee their entire chain's operation. Cody's company had a reputation for high-tech security and surveillance. He'd coupled his father's military training and expertise with his keen sense of business during the past ten years and had built a respected multimillion-dollar company equal to none. Trent already had a small team from Landon's agency working for him at the hotel and they'd installed security measures on the grounds before the hotel had opened.

"I heard rumors you were thinking of taking a backseat in your company." Trent leaned back in his chair, wondering why the hell Code had really come to babysit a celebrity starlet.

Code's mouth quirked up. "Did you hear that from your brother?"

"Brock?" Trent scratched the back of his head trying to recall. "Yeah, maybe."

"I might have said that at one time, after a few too many drinks," he admitted with a wry expression. "My work consumes all my time, leaving no room for anything else."

Trent could relate to that. He'd been solidly consumed with the hotels for years, but Tempest West was his baby and he'd eaten, slept and breathed it for months now. Nothing was more important than seeing to its success.

"Hell, I'm not complaining, but why you? You could have sent any number of the experts on your team? We have your security in place, we just needed a little extra insurance, is all."

"Maybe I wanted to see Tempest West myself. Maybe I miss working in the field. Maybe I like country music."

Maybe none of the above, Trent thought. There was another reason that Cody Landon had come to Tempest West and he doubted he'd find the true reason until Code decided he wanted him to know.

"Fair enough. You know Sarah Rose arrived this morning. We want to make her stay here as uncomplicated as possible, so the security around her will be subtle but effective. Our anniversary celebration starts in one week, by invitation only. Sarah's presence here was our main draw. She'll do several intimate shows weekly, up at the lake. We've screened the guests and shouldn't have a problem with anyone. We're hoping the hotel sells out."

"We *are* sold out," Julia said. She was standing at the office threshold wearing a smug expression and an ivory two-piece suit that accentuated her curves and showed off her long legs. Delicate skin peeked out from under the V of her jacket's wide lapel, showing just enough cleavage to make Trent swallow hard. Having Julia deliver the news that Tempest West was sold out only intensified his desire for her.

She walked into the office, offering her hand to Code. "I'm Julia Lowell. Sorry I wasn't here when you arrived."

Code stood and took a long assessing look at Julia. "Worth the wait, Miss Lowell," he said, shaking her hand. "We've spoken on the phone."

"Yes," she said with a smile, "we have."

Julia finished briefing him and when she questioned him about coming personally, teasing that she hoped he wouldn't charge them head-honcho fees, Code's reply to her was just as cryptic as it had been to Trent.

He gave nothing away.

"I'm hosting dinner with Sarah Rose in my suite later tonight. Trent will be there as well. It would be a good chance for you to meet her. Would you care to join us?" she asked.

Code didn't hesitate. "Thank you."

Julia added, "Sarah's had a very busy, trying year. She wants to keep a low profile. I think she's exhausted both mentally and physically. She's here alone, no entourage, no business manager. I got the feeling she hasn't had much privacy lately. It's our hope that she enjoys herself at Tempest West enough to want to return for other exclusive engagements."

Unmoved, Code's expression didn't change, except for the slightest flicker in his eyes. "I've got a file on her. You're right, she's had quite a year," he agreed, his mouth curling with a slight twist. "I'll check in with my security team and then meet you for dinner."

Julia nodded. "Eight o'clock. I'm staying in the Palomino Suite in the main hotel."

Once Code exited the office, Trent grinned wide and took Julia's hand, pulling her close. "We're sold out?"

He was in the mood to celebrate.

"For three full weeks and the reservation desk is still ringing off the hook. I'd venture to guess we'll have every room, suite and cottage full for the entire month. It seems," she added, "the private invitations did the trick. Didn't seem to matter that we nearly doubled our room fees."

"It's all due to your hard work, darlin'. You managed to pull it off." Trent circled his hands around her waist, coming face-to-face with her, breathing in her erotic scent and itching to do more than hold her.

"I just figured out what your clientele really wanted. Then I gave it to them."

"Have I told you how amazing you are?"

"Am I?"

Julia got that wary look in her eyes again. Telling her he cared for her wouldn't come off as sounding sincere now. In truth, the woman had begun to really matter to him, although she didn't trust him, and Trent couldn't push her too hard. He couldn't afford to lose her. He needed her at Tempest West. "You're my miracle worker."

Julia lowered her head and nodded. "Just doing my job, Trent." She backed away and gazed at him with accusation in her eyes. "What you hired me to do, remember?"

Ouch. Trent knew enough to back off from that look. She still hadn't forgiven him for the way he'd manipulated her employment here. But he had to give her credit for doing a damn fine job here. Even though she'd resented him, she hadn't let that get in the way of turning things around at Tempest West.

He had to admire that.

"Yeah, but you deserve something more from me."

Julia's pretty grass-green eyes widened. "More from you?"

He nodded. "A bonus. When all is said and done, I'd planned on giving you—"

Julia's eyes narrowed, like a suspicious cat. "Are you talking about a *monetary* bonus, Trent?"

Trent nodded. "Sure enough."

Julia's mouth formed a perfectly round O. Her expression registered disappointment for a moment. She inhaled slowly and whispered, "Make sure it's a good one, Trent. Lord knows I deserve it for putting up with you."

Then she turned on her heels and exited his office, slamming the door behind her.

Julia paced her suite, trembling with mounting fury at Trent. She uttered more than a few unkind words aimed solely at the cowboy. She couldn't believe him. Had their time together meant nothing to him?

Didn't he know that the *more* she wanted from him had nothing to do with contracts and money? Didn't he know that she was working exceptionally hard to forgive his deceit and learn to trust him?

Was *everything* he did related to his precious hotel?

Julia had always known the answer, but deep in her heart, she yearned for that something *more* with Trent. Deep in her heart, she knew that she wanted a future with him, the proverbial *happily ever after.*

But Trent only saw her as a commodity, a means to keep Tempest West in the black. A way to ensure besting his brother Brock with their crazy challenge.

"You're a fool, Trent," she muttered. She walked from the bedroom to the parlor and back with the intent of tidying up for dinner but accomplished nothing. She fell onto the bed as tears rolled down her cheeks.

Trent was tossing away something more precious than his hotel. She knew it, but doubted he could see past his own aspirations to recognize it.

"Dense, insensitive, arrogant," she whispered before surrendering to her sudden fatigue. She closed her eyes and rested, refusing to worry about her dinner party tonight. She had a few hours to nap and darn if she didn't deserve a break.

Four hours later, Julia reassembled her thoughts and, feeling slightly renewed from her rest, decided she wouldn't give Trent the satisfaction of knowing how much he'd hurt her. Actually, once she reasoned it out, she realized that offering to reward her efforts was sound business. She'd accept the bonus graciously because she had worked very hard and deserved every cent.

Julia dressed in a sweeping black dress of chiffon and black satin. She put on chandelier rhinestone earrings and let her dark hair fall freely in subtle waves onto her shoulders. She puckered up and outlined her lips with daring red, then put a touch of green shadow on her eyelids.

Once the table by the balcony was dressed, she dismissed the staff and walked to Sarah's suite on the far edge of the property. She knocked and Sarah opened the door timidly then smiled with relief when she saw it was Julia and exited closing the door behind her. "I'm ready."

Sarah's aqua eyes were brighter and her face appeared more relaxed than hours earlier when she'd arrived at the hotel. "That was the best six hours I've spent in a long time."

"Really? What did you do?" Julia asked as they walked along the path leading to the main hotel.

"I took a long soak in the tub. I read. I napped. No phone calls. No text messages. I shut off my cell." She grinned. "It was heaven."

"It can be like that every day. We'll make sure of it."

Sarah, wearing a pretty dotted Swiss eyelet dress, looking like the embodiment of a simple country girl and not the flashy, sequined, studded star she usually portrayed, appeared happy. "A girl could get spoiled."

"You haven't seen nothin' yet," Julia teased. They entered her suite and took a seat in the parlor, chatting about the Dream Foundation and what they'd both planned on accomplishing next for the charity during the upcoming holidays.

"I've got a concert series planned in New Orleans with all proceeds going to the foundation. We're going to make some dreams come true for Katrina victims. Many children and their families still are displaced."

When a knock sounded at her door, Julia rose and took a deep breath, preparing to see Trent for the first time since their exchange hours ago. "That'll be Trent Tyler, the mastermind of Tempest West. And he's bringing along the head of security. I hope you don't mind. Trent and I felt you should meet. We think it's necessary for your added safety."

Sarah rose from her seat. "That's fine, Julia. I don't want my presence here to upset the order of things. Unfortunately, I'm used to extra security."

When Trent and Cody Landon entered, Julia faced them both graciously, but when she turned around to give the introductions, Sarah took one look at Cody and her expression crumbled. It appeared it took all of her courage to keep from stumbling back into her seat.

"Hello, Sarah," Landon said, without introduction.

"Code," she offered, their gazes locked.

It was as if Julia and Trent weren't in the room. After a brief awkward silence, Sarah composed herself with poise and explained that she and Cody Landon had been childhood friends back in Texas. They hadn't seen each other in ten years. *Friends* being an understatement,

Julia assessed, but neither one of them elaborated about their relationship.

Sarah kept her composure throughout dinner, even though Code never took his eyes off her. After coffee and dessert, Code offered to walk Sarah Rose back to her cottage suite and Sarah agreed.

"I didn't know they knew each other," Trent said after they'd left.

"Obviously, he didn't want us to know. Must be a good reason. I'll talk to Sarah tomorrow and make sure she's okay with it."

"Good idea," he said, walking over to the balcony window and looking out, his hands thrust in the pockets of his trousers. The room fell silent. Then he turned around, meeting her gaze, his dark eyes intent on hers. "I also didn't know offering you a bonus would upset you, darlin'. I'm proud of you and wanted to show it."

Trent's abundant charm could sway a rattlesnake and right now, Julia felt enough like a reptile to want to crawl away on her belly. She'd behaved like a shrew earlier when Trent only wanted to thank her for her hard work. He was her boss, after all.

The tall, lean sexy cowboy wore a sincere expression and her heart did a little flip. Julia remembered Laney's words—to fight for Trent and go after what she wanted. She shrugged and cast aside her stubborn pride to offer up the truth. "I guess I wanted more from you, Trent."

Trent stepped away from the window to face her, his eyes dark with question. "For weeks, you've been pushing me away. I haven't looked at another woman since we met and you know I want you." He put a finger to her cheek, sliding his finger down along the line of her face in a caressing way that made her bones melt.

"You and me, we can set fire to that bed in there, darlin'." He slid his finger down her throat, then outlined her bare shoulder. "We can have a great time together."

He hooked his finger under the strap of her dress and lowered it down. "You're beautiful, Julia. And smart."

He kissed her shoulder, his lips lingering. Julia's throat went dry.

"I've got nothing but admiration for you."

He kissed her again, pressing his lips a little lower, near the V of her neckline. "I want you every way a man can want a woman."

He lowered the neckline, releasing material to bare the upper part of her breast. Then he kissed her there and Julia's resistance disintegrated. "And then ten times more."

"Trent," she whispered, "I don't know if I can trust you."

Slowly, he lowered the straps off her shoulders and her dress flowed down to her waist. Cool night air caressed her breasts. "I'm asking that you do." With that, he lifted her up into his arms and carried her to the bedroom. She roped her arms automatically around his neck. Their eyes met, his heavy-lidded and ablaze with desire. Her heart pounded. Fast and strong, it thumped inside her chest.

Gently, he laid her down on the bed, her dress

flowing in folds around her hips. He stood over her, his jaw tight, his gaze intent and his body erect. "Tell me what you want, honey."

Oh, God. Julia knew what she wanted, but short of ordering him to love her, she couldn't voice her heart-felt desires. She wanted this man beside her for life. She wanted to bear his children and grow old with him.

She wanted to trust him.

The debate in her mind lasted for half a second. She couldn't turn Trent away. She ached for his kiss. She needed his hands on her, making her feel beautiful and desired. She wanted him inside her, the thought of him making love to her too powerful to deny.

She rolled onto her side and pointed. "Take off your shirt."

Trent's brows rose provocatively and his lips quirked up. He undid his shirt slowly, each button he unfastened allowing her a heady show of his tanned, broad chest. Once done, he dropped the shirt to the ground and stared at her.

"Now, the boots, cowboy."

He sat on the edge of the bed and removed his snake-skin boots. He lined them up neatly and the vision those boots made standing tall by the side of her four-poster bed touched a deep sentimental chord within her.

Still sitting on the bed, he faced her. "I don't strip down to my skivvies on command for *just* anyone, Julia."

"Meaning, you use discretion?"

"Meaning," he said, "I'd only do it for you."

Julia grinned and her heart skipped a beat. "Really? I wouldn't have guessed."

But Julia knew Trent wasn't a player or a flirt. He didn't seem to have a long list of women in his past. She believed him when he said he used discretion and that was one trait she found extremely endearing about him.

He grabbed her legs just above the ankles and gently pulled her toward him, bedsheets and all. "Now you know," he said, bending down to plant a heart-stopping kiss on her mouth. She craved the familiar taste of him and as she breathed in his powerful earthy scent a little gasp of pleasure escaped her throat. Trent smiled. "You're important to me, darlin'."

Looking up, Julia stared into sincere dark incredible eyes. "Make love to me, Trent."

"You won't have to ask twice."

He removed her dress, helping as she wiggled her hips and shimmied out of it. Next he slipped a finger under her black satin thong and removed it, leaving her completely naked. He looked as though he'd devour her. Instead of taking her in another earth-shattering kiss, he lifted her hips, situated her legs on his shoulders, centering his hot mouth between her thighs, and brought her quick and complete satisfaction with the stroking of his tongue. Her orgasm shattered her and left her breathing hard, desperately clutching his shoulders.

"Oh...Trent," she breathed out.

He rose and removed his pants, then came to her again, kissing her thoroughly, caressing her breasts and suckling on each supple tip until she wanted to scream out her pleasure.

He touched every inch of her, his hands roaming and staking their claim. Her skin heated. Her body trembled. Every cell in her body craved him and ached for more.

Laying her flat under him on the bed, he rose over her and thrust inside her, his silken erection thick and hard. He moved slowly, a torturous thrust that brought fevered anticipation and pure lust. He thrust farther and she wrapped herself around him, each second escalating with fiery expectation.

Heavy-lidded, Trent watched her, his jaw tight, the strength and breadth of him being tested by sheer will. He was so powerful, so strong and so incredibly beautiful to Julia she wanted to cry.

He rasped, "We're gonna catch fire, now, honey. Ready?"

Julia swallowed and nodded.

Then Trent did what he did best.

And they exploded into flames.

Nine

Julia woke up the next morning from a blissful sleep. She knew instinctively that Trent would be gone from her bed. Sunshine poured into her window. It was well past dawn and he was probably hard at work in his office by now.

Her body sated from two incredible bouts of love-making last night, she really shouldn't complain, but just once she wished she could wake up with Trent beside her. She'd inflicted a self-imposed rule of secrecy. It wouldn't do her any good for the employees to know that she was sleeping with the boss.

Julia hugged her pillow to her chest wishing it were Trent. Then she glanced at the empty half of the bed and saw a small envelope with the Tempest West logo on it on the other pillow, her name written across the center.

She smiled, recognizing Trent's handwriting. Sitting up, she opened the envelope and read the card silently.

You destroyed me last night. We're good together. Sleep in. I'll see you later.
Trent

Julia folded the note back into the envelope and got out of bed. Setting the note in her dresser drawer, she let out a deep sigh. They were hardly the words of love she'd wanted to hear, but she considered the note progress since Trent had never left her one before.

Julia stepped into the shower and lingered, enjoying the warm spray of water raining down. She shampooed and conditioned her hair then used the loofah on her body. She lathered herself with delicate gardenia-scented soap and rinsed, feeling revitalized and refreshed.

Trent hadn't been the only one destroyed. A night in bed with Trent meant a vigorous workout and Julia wished she could sleep away the day, reliving the intense sensations he elicited in her. But duty called. Julia had work to do and she'd already wasted away part of the morning.

Feeling carefree, she dressed in a floral skirt in hues of lavender and rose and donned a solid matching knit sweater. She put on her favorite jewelry—a drop necklace and small diamond earrings. After ten minutes with the curling iron, her hair fell in soft curls around her face and she had the look she wanted to face the day.

She didn't know where her relationship with Trent was going, but today, she wouldn't worry about it. She'd pretty much decided to live in the moment and leave her concerns behind.

Ten minutes later, she knocked on Sarah Rose's door, ready to give her a tour of Tempest West as promised. Sarah opened the door dressed in ivory silk pajamas, her auburn hair disheveled and looking as if she'd just gotten out of bed.

"Good morning," Julia said, keeping her questions to herself for now.

"Is it?"

Sarah's cryptic remark had Julia raising an eyebrow. "If this is a bad time, I can come back later." Then she amended, "Or we don't have to do this at all today."

Sarah opened the door wider. "Come in, Julia. I'm sorry. I'm a little out of sorts. I didn't sleep much last night."

"Oh, I'm sorry to hear that. Were you uncomfortable? Is there anything here that doesn't meet with your approval?"

Sarah waved her off with a smile. "Don't be silly. I'm not a diva. The accommodations here are just as perfect as can be. I couldn't approve more. Of *them*."

Then she plopped onto the butter-yellow leather sofa and shrugged. "Other things kept me awake last night."

Julia had a feeling she knew where this was going.

"Uh-oh. Was it Cody Landon? Let me say no one was more surprised than Trent and I that you two knew each other. I hope he didn't upset you… We can make other arrange—"

Sarah put her hand up. "Julia. Wait. Don't make assumptions on my behalf. I'm doing just fine. I knew I might run into him one day. Please don't feel you need to go making other arrangements," she said softly, her southern twang coming through. "Seeing him here just caught me by surprise."

"I saw your reaction to him, Sarah." Julia sat down beside her and turned to face her directly. Sarah had nearly crumpled for a second when she'd first laid eyes on Code. Not that he wasn't extremely handsome, dressed in devastating black from head to toe, his face covered in day-old scruff with those incredible deep sea-blue eyes landing on Sarah and staying there all during dinner.

Sarah closed her eyes briefly. "Code and I…well, we knew each other a long time ago."

"I'm here to listen, if you need someone. But don't feel you have to say anything at all."

Sarah smiled warmly. "Thank you. But it doesn't matter anymore, Julia. It's old news and not very exciting at that," she offered on a deep sigh. "If you give me twenty minutes, I'll be ready for the tour of the grounds." She dismissed the subject that easily, but Julia knew there was much more going on than Sarah wanted to admit.

"Why don't you stay and have something to eat while I shower and dress?"

Julia looked over at the granite counter filled with goodies. "Thank you. I'll have some strawberries and coffee and wait for you outside on the deck."

Twenty minutes later, Julia took a camouflaged Sarah Rose, dressed in dark sunglasses and a ponytail covered with a Dallas Cowboys ball cap, out on an hour tour of the grounds. Proudly, she showed Trent's hotel off and drove the perimeter in the Jeep, making their last stop at Destiny Lake.

"This is it," she said to Sarah. "We'll set you up on the dock and put our guests in seats just a few feet away, no more than three hundred seats in all. There'll be no hoopla, no flashing lights, no backup singers. Just an intimate evening with you and your fans."

Sarah took off her sunglasses to take it all in, her gaze lingering on the glistening lake. "I can barely recall singing to a small audience. I miss it. I like the dock idea."

"Afterward, if you don't mind, maybe you can shake a few hands, sign some autographs in a little postshow party at the hotel. You'll have the utmost in security the entire time."

"That's fine with me. I won't tell my manager though. He'd be on the first plane out here. I trust you, Julia. And I'm looking forward to this."

"Thank you. We won't let you down. We want this to be a pleasant experience for you as well as our guests."

"I think it will be," she acknowledged, but her voice was laced with trepidation and Julia believed it all had to do with Code Landon.

* * *

When Julia walked into his office, Trent was knee-deep in work, his head down as he concentrated on hotel projections. "Kim, can you bring me last month's reports?"

"It's not Kim," Julia said, closing the door and walking toward his desk.

Trent abandoned his work long enough to glance up. Her heart tumbled when he lost his all-business expression to smile at her. "Wow." He rose from his seat and approached her. "You look prettier than sunshine." He took her hand, pulled her up close and kissed her. "Taste sweet as sugar, too."

"Flattery, Mr. Tyler?"

"Just plain fact."

Julia stroked his jaw, enjoying the freedom to touch him now. She'd resisted him for weeks and now she couldn't get enough. She lifted up on her toes and kissed him back.

"Glad you got your facts straight."

He grinned then glanced at the files behind him on his desk. "I got a pile of work to do today. Appreciate you interrupting, though. It's good to see you." Then he nuzzled her neck. "You okay, after last night?"

The reminder of their hot night of sex stalled her breath. She whispered, "Don't I look okay?"

Trent skimmed his hands down her back, tugged up the hem of her skirt and cupped her derriere. Fiery signals went off in her body.

"Hell, Julia. I've got a meeting in half an hour and

I'm not nearly ready or I'd show you how *okay* you look right now."

Caught up in Trent's caresses, she fumbled with her next thought. "Sorry, but…I, uh…came in here for a reason. It's business, but it can wait. I'll leave you to get your work done."

With reluctance, she pulled away from him, only to have him catch her and draw her back with his hands firmly on her backside. "Trent," she breathed out.

He stared deep into her eyes. "Meet me tonight. Come out to my house. I want you there with me."

Julia swallowed and nodded slowly, looking at him as she backed out of his reach.

"Seven o'clock. Don't be late."

Julia walked out of his office, her mind giddy, her legs weak and her heart joyfully thrumming.

There was no point being coy with Trent. Julia knew what he liked and she was darn sure going to please him tonight. She put on her striking fuchsia Zac Posen dress, something she kept for special occasions, slipped her feet into black two-inch heels and accented her outfit with thin black pearls, teardrop earrings and about a dozen narrow bangle bracelets.

She put her hair up in a sophisticated do, securing the tresses with an onyx-beaded comb. Glancing in the mirror, she gave a quick nod of approval at the image reflecting back. Picking up her handbag, she exited her suite.

She'd made plans for Kim and Sarah to have a light

supper together, so that Kim could go over some "details" about her performances. Julia smiled as Kim's stunned expression flashed in her mind.

"You want me to have dinner with Sarah? Just the two of us?" Kim had asked.

"Yes, I think she'd enjoy meeting you. And you'd be doing me a big favor," she'd said.

Not that Julia had planned on babysitting Sarah for her entire stay at Tempest West, but after their conversation today she thought Sarah might like a few hours of distraction. And Julia would sleep better knowing she wouldn't have to worry about Sarah's activities tonight.

That's if Julia got any sleep at all this evening. She couldn't help but grin at the notion.

Trent left word that the Jeep would be at her disposal tonight and apologized for not picking her up. Her rule, not his, he reminded her.

Julia drove the distance to Trent's house on the grounds, commending herself on her memory. When the house came into view, she parked the car and exited, staring at the rustic porch and smoke pumping out of the chimney. The cozy, intimate setting invited warmth and she couldn't wait for their night to begin. A thrill coursed through her system as she approached the front door.

She knocked and waited.

Then knocked again. "Trent?" she called out.

Trent finally answered the door, his cell phone to his ear. "Yes, that's right. I need to fly out tonight. As soon as you can get the plane ready."

He gestured for Julia to come in. Her heart in her throat, she entered, seeing candles lit on the mantel of the fireplace, on the dining table and in every feasible corner. A beautiful yellow-gold hue filled the room. Three arrangements of red roses with delicate baby's breath filled cut crystal vases, the sweet scent lingering in the air.

As Trent spoke on the phone, he took up a poker and broke up the fire in the hearth the best he could. Next, he went around the room blowing out all the candles until only the setting sun brought light into the room.

Once his conversation was over, he flipped off the phone and walked over to her. "Sorry, Julia." He took hold of her hand. "Evan called just a few minutes ago. Laney went into premature labor."

Julia gasped. "Oh, no. It's too soon. She's not due for months."

"Laney's blood pressure skyrocketed and it's touch and go."

Julia's breath caught. Horribly shocked, she asked, *"Touch and go?* You mean Laney's in danger?"

"Very much so. Both of them are. I've never heard Evan so frantic." Trent rubbed the back of his neck and spoke with deep concern. "I put the manager in charge of the hotel. My pilot is fueling up the jet. I've got to get there. Evan needs me."

"I'm going, too," she said adamantly, not waiting for an invitation. Panic knotted up her stomach. "I have to see Laney." Tears stung her eyes and she barely got the words out. "She wants this baby so much, Trent."

"I know. They both do."

"Do I have time to pack a bag?" she asked.

He shook his head. "No, I'll grab you a jacket and we'll get you whatever you need once we arrive in L.A. We have to get to the airfield."

Trent walked briskly into his room and came out with a tan suede jacket and a small duffel bag for himself. He placed the jacket around her shoulders. It was huge on her, yet wearing it brought her a measure of comfort. He tugged it close and kissed her forehead. "Ready?"

She gave a slow nod, filled with fear for her best friend. "Let's go."

Shortly after, they arrived in Los Angeles. A driver met them and drove them straight to the hospital. They rushed inside and Trent immediately spoke with the unit nurse who had given them very little information.

No change.

Evan Tyler was with his wife.

After half an hour of waiting silently, Trent pacing and Julia near tears, Evan finally walked into the room. Trent greeted him immediately and they embraced, hugging tight, but Julia stayed back. Seeing Evan's haggard face, his eyes bloodshot and his body sagging frightened her more than getting the news so unexpectedly earlier.

Dear God, Julia pleaded, let everything be okay.

"There's no change," he said.

Julia rose to give Evan a big hug. "I'm so sorry.

Laney looked so healthy when she was in Arizona with all of us. Do they know what caused it?"

Weary, Evan ran his hands down his face, shaking his head. "No one knows. Sometimes, this sort of thing happens. She'd been feeling great yesterday. We'd just finished setting up the nursery and she was so happy. When she woke up after a nap this afternoon, she felt weak and then started cramping up. That's all I know. I rushed her here and…and…"

Julia took Evan's hand. "She's going to come through this. I know it, Evan. My best friend is strong."

Evan nodded in agreement, yet the fear in his eyes belied his optimism. He turned to Trent. "Did you call Mom?"

"Yes, I told her to sit tight and I'll keep her posted."

"You think she'll do that?" Evan asked.

Trent's lips quirked up briefly. "Hell, no. She'll be on the first plane out. I'm surprised she didn't beat us here."

"Me, too," Evan said with love in his eyes.

"You look tired as hell. Sit down. I'll get you something to eat," Trent said.

"No, I can't take the time. I need to get back in there."

"Come on, Ev. Won't do Laney any good if you faint dead away."

"Just coffee," Evan said firmly, pointing to a two-pot coffee warmer in the corner of the waiting room.

"Right, just coffee. That'll keep your strength up," Trent said wryly, but he strode briskly over to the table and poured two cups of coffee into foam cups. He handed Evan one, and Julia the other.

"Let's all sit for a minute," Trent said calmly. "Julia's exhausted."

Julia opened her mouth to protest, but when Trent gave her a warning look, she realized his intent. Evan would sit down on her behalf if he believed she needed the rest.

Julia plopped down in a chair and Evan and Trent flanked her on both sides. She sipped the strong bitter coffee that had probably been sitting in the pot most of the day. Evan took a few large gulps quietly, resting for only a minute, and then he got up abruptly. "I've got to check on my wife."

Trent rose, too. "I'm here, if you need anything."

"I know. I can always count on you, Trent," Evan said, in a fatherly way.

Julia stood and hugged Evan again, wordlessly giving him her support.

Once he left the room, Trent took one look at her and frowned. "You're trembling."

"I'm scared." Her eyes misted up again and she struggled to hold back tears.

Trent lifted the suede jacket she'd discarded earlier from her chair and draped it onto her shoulders. Tugging her close, he wrapped his arms around her, tucking her head under his chin, and held her tight for a long time. They just stood there in the middle of the waiting room like that.

Cocooned in his strength, Julia closed her eyes and prayed for the innocent baby and for her best friend's safety. After a time, Trent helped her to a seat and she snuggled in his warmth and dozed lightly, drifting in and out, faintly hearing hospital sounds, soft conversations and an occasional dinging of the elevator. All the while, Trent held her to him and it was well past midnight when Evan emerged from Laney's room.

Trent nudged her gently and she lifted from her position on his chest.

"Laney's blood pressure is better, but not completely under control," Evan said. "They gave her a sedative for sleep. The baby is hanging on," Evan said, his voice slightly hopeful. "I won't leave her. I'm set up in her room. You two need to get some rest. I'll call you in the morning and let you know how she's doing."

"You're sure? We can stay?" Trent spoke for both of them.

"I'm sure." Evan looked her way. "You need to take Julia home."

"Promise you'll call if there's any change?" Julia asked, hating to leave the hospital.

"I promise. There's nothing you can do tonight. Come back in the morning." He reached into his pocket and tossed Trent his keys. "Take my car."

Trent tightened his grip on Julia's shoulder, nodding. "We'll be back early."

Ten

As Trent drove Julia to her apartment, she stared straight ahead, overwhelmed by emotion and fear. It didn't seem fair after all Evan and Laney had gone through to finally be a family to have this happen to them. Their beginning had been tumultuous at best and Laney thought she'd never come to trust Evan. Now, she trusted him with her life. And their precious innocent baby was struggling to survive, as well.

Julia drew in a big breath and sighed, her exhaustion weakening her resolve to be strong. She fought off tears every moment while in the hospital, but she couldn't seem to hold them back any longer. They trickled down her cheeks.

Trent reached over to cover his hand over hers on the seat. The simple tender gesture touched something deep inside and she glanced his way, her heart warming.

Concern evident on his face, he turned to flash her a quick smile then squeezed her hand a little tighter.

They drove the rest of the way in silence. He pulled up in front of her apartment building, turned off the engine and leaned toward her. Using the pads of his thumbs, he wiped the moisture off her cheeks gently. Before she could thank him, he bounded out of the car and came around her side to open the door.

When she stepped onto the sidewalk, he took her hand and walked her to her apartment door. "Are you going to be all right tonight?"

Julia blinked and realized that Trent didn't intend to stay. "I…" she began, then because she wasn't into playing games, she gave him the truth. "I don't want to be alone, Trent." She wanted to be with him. Nestled in his strength. Cuddled in his heat. Sheltered, comforted and safe. "I want you to stay with me."

Trent nodded. "Okay, darlin'. Didn't want to inter-fere with your sleep, is all. You've had a long night."

"I'll sleep better knowing you're here."

"You saying I'm better than a warm glass of milk?"

"And counting sheep," she bantered, enjoying a moment of levity as she pushed the key into the lock and opened her apartment door. "Here we are," she said.

Julia loved her apartment and how sunlight cast soft hues into the rooms during the day and moonlight added a warm romantic glow at night. Her apartment held a certain feminine appeal, yet the textures and solid furniture made it a place a man could feel comfortable in as well.

Trent followed her inside, his gaze quickly touring the living room. "I remember. Nice place. Didn't get out of the bedroom much, though. Did we?"

Smitten with the striking Texas cowboy from the get-go, Julia had gone into that short affair after Laney's wedding one hundred percent. Steady, efficient, cautious Julia usually didn't get blindsided that way. But at the time, Trent had simply been her best friend's new brother-in-law. They'd clicked like two magnets, drawn together by an irresistible force.

"No," she answered, recalling how wantonly she'd behaved, making love with an unquenchable thirst to a near total stranger. Heat crawled up her neck and she changed the subject. "Are you hungry?"

"No." He walked over to her and immediately lifted her into his arms. He carried her to the bedroom. "You're hitting the sack, darlin'. We both need sleep."

He set her down carefully and kissed her quickly, then placed both hands on her shoulders and pivoted her around. He spoke very close to her ear, his hot breath a whisper on her throat. He began to unzip her dress. "When I pictured doing this, it wasn't to get you into bed to *sleep*."

She turned her head to look at him. "You pictured doing this?"

Trent laughed softly. "Even before I saw you in this knockout dress, I pictured undressing you. Yeah." He nipped at her bare shoulder and stroked her tenderly. Then with a resigned sigh, he ordered, "Now hop into bed." He turned around and headed toward the door.

"Where are you going?" she asked.

"I need a drink. Your liquor in the same place, darlin'?"

She nodded, holding her dress to her chest. "Beer's in the fridge. Whiskey's on the bar." Then before exiting the room, Julia called to him. "Trent?"

"Hmm?"

"They're going to be okay, right?"

"My gut's saying yes." He winked. "Get into bed. I'll be back in a minute."

He clicked off the light, leaving Julia alone. She tossed and turned for fifteen minutes. Only when Trent stripped down to his boxers and joined her in bed did she finally settle down a little.

"I thought you'd be asleep by now," he said quietly, sliding close beside her.

"I can't sleep. I'm so worried."

Trent wrapped his arms around her. "I am, too, but we won't be good to anyone without some shut-eye."

Julia giggled softly.

"What?"

"You're such a cowboy, Trent Tyler."

"You like cowboys," he stated unequivocally.

A deep sigh escaped. "Lucky for you."

"I am lucky. Now…shh. Go to sleep, darlin'." He snuggled her closer and stroked her hair, caressing her into sweet oblivion.

"I don't know what I'd do without you here," she said, resting her head against his shoulder.

"Glad to oblige," he said, in a contrived, heavy Texas accent.

Julia smiled and laid her head on his chest, setting her hand on his torso. She didn't just *like* cowboys.

She loved them.

This one in particular.

There was no use denying it any longer.

Trent woke as dawn broke through the plantation-style shutters, filtering an early haze of light into the bedroom. Julia still slept, her head on his chest.

This was a record first in Trent's life. He'd never slept with a woman without making love to her. He'd never allowed himself to get deeply involved with anyone. It seemed that he'd always had something to prove. When he was younger, he was constantly competing with Brock. As the youngest of the boys, he'd needed to keep up, to show his parents that he was just as strong, just as capable, just as worthy of their love.

After his father died tragically, he'd felt lost and abandoned for a time. But Evan had been there to take up the slack and he found that he didn't want to be coddled by his mother anymore. He'd wanted the same respect his mother had for Evan.

And most recently, he'd had this amazing vision of Tempest West, something both of his brothers failed to believe in. He'd spent the majority of his time and energy pouring himself into the project.

Its success was an integral part of him.

Then Julia entered his life, the woman who could turn his failing enterprise around. He'd needed her savvy and marketing skills and wasn't one bit remorseful at the way that had come about. He'd do it again in a New York second.

In bed, Julia compared to no other woman he'd been with. They connected on the highest level and turned each other inside out.

So when Julia told him he was lucky, he could only agree. And he'd do everything in his power to keep luck on his side.

She shifted on his chest, her breath warm and inviting. Trent groaned and thought about a cold shower and the woman in his arms.

Julia had been so vulnerable last night. She'd been scared, worried and restless, and he found he wanted to simply hold her, comfort her and help her fall asleep. An odd sensation swept through him and luckily—*again*—for him, Julia took that moment to rouse from her sleep, keeping him from having to define his wandering emotions.

"Mmm…" she muttered, waking and lifting her head from his chest. "This is nice."

Trent caught sight of the shimmering nightie dipping

low on her chest, allowing him a sneak peek at her full breasts. "What is?"

She smiled, her eyes dewy and heavy-lidded. "Waking up with you."

Trent liked the thought of that too much. Right now, he liked everything about Julia. He leaned in for a quick kiss. "We'd better get a move on, darlin', or in another second, I won't let you outta this bed."

Julia glanced where his gaze had roamed and straightened out her skimpy nightgown. "Oh." Then she refocused her attention. "You're right. I'll put coffee on while you shower. We can get to the hospital before seven, if we hurry."

Less than an hour later, Trent put his hand to Julia's back and guided her to the hospital waiting room only to find his mother there, sitting next to Matthew Lowell.

"Dad?" Julia said, darting glances from her father to Trent's mother.

"Rebecca called me last night in a panic. I picked her up this morning at the airport."

"Hi, Mom," Trent said, kissing his mother on the cheek and holding back a grin as he watched Matthew explain himself to his daughter.

"Hello, Mrs. Tyler," Julia said graciously and he mentally commended her on making a quick recovery from seeing her father with his mother again. "How is Laney? The baby?"

"Still no change, I'm afraid," his mother replied, her eyes swollen from fatigue and maybe a few tears. "Evan said she rested a little, but if they can't get her blood pressure under control, they might have to take the baby by cesarean section."

Trent noted fright and apprehension on his mother's face. She'd lost her husband at a young age and raised three boys on her own. It hadn't always been easy, but she'd been there, through thick and thin. Now, she feared for Laney, for her firstborn son and for the new grandchild she'd wanted for years. "The baby is a Tyler. He'll come through this, Mom. He's strong. Probably as stubborn as Evan. And as tough."

Rebecca took his hand. "You're right, Trent. My sons were strong and healthy. You're all fighters." The notion sat well with his mother and she relaxed a little.

"I bet none of you have eaten a thing. I'll call in for breakfast." Trent flipped his phone on and called Tempest Los Angeles. He spoke directly to the hotel chef and ordered enough food to sustain them through most of the day, making sure it would be delivered hot and fresh.

"There's some tables out on the patio. We'll sit down and eat when the food comes. I'll leave word with the nurse where we'll be. I'm going to see if I can get someone to drag Evan out for a bite."

A short while later, Trent sat at a patio table with Julia, both of their parents and, remarkably, he was able to get Evan to agree to have some breakfast. Evan's Tempest staff had worked extra hard, delivering a wide array of food in a quick span of time for their employer. Trent thanked them all and handed them a big tip.

"The good news is that they've gotten Laney's blood pressure down," Evan said, wolfing down eggs Benedict and coffee as if it was his last meal. "The contractions have stopped." Evan inhaled sharply and shook his head as if the thought of what might have happened quaked him. He finished off his coffee. "Laney's very tired now, but she wants to see all of you later."

"Oh, that's good," his mother said, slightly relieved, as she set down her fork. She was a slender woman who ate very little, so Trent was glad to see she'd eaten her entire breakfast.

"I can't wait to see her," Julia added, her voice much lighter than before. "She's had us all worried."

"Laney's like my second daughter," Matthew said. "The two girls have been like sisters. I've been sending up some heavy prayers for that child and her baby."

"You and me both. I've never felt so damn helpless in my life," Evan said, rising from the table. "Thanks for being here. It means a lot. I'll let you know something more as soon as the doctor examines Laney again."

Evan turned to him. "Walk back with me, Trent."

"Sure thing." Absently, Trent leaned over to plant a quick kiss on Julia's cheek. "I'll be back soon."

Julia darted a glance at both parents, then cast him a sheepish smile before he walked off.

They headed toward the elevator. "I can't thank you enough for coming and taking care of things," Evan said. "Brock's halfway between New Orleans and Maui right now. He said he'd come, but I told him to hold off.

It's good you're here for Mom. She's more fragile than she looks."

"You've got your hands full, Ev. You take care of your wife and baby. I'll handle the rest."

"I appreciate that." They stopped at the elevator and Evan laid a hand on his shoulder and looked him square in the eyes. "Julia's a great girl, Trent. Not only is she Laney's best friend, but I've gotten to know her some myself."

"Yeah, I agree. Your point?"

"Women like that don't usually walk into your life. Take it from an expert. Laney and I almost didn't make it. Now, I can't imagine my life without her. Nothing's more important than what we have together. If that girl means something to you, let her know. That's all I'm saying." Evan punched the elevator button. "Think about it."

When the elevator dinged, Evan stepped inside and the doors closed automatically. Trent stood there for a minute, staring at the elevator door, his brother's words ringing in his ear.

"Excuse me, mister," an older woman said, trying to get to the elevator button.

Trent stepped out of her way, mumbling, "Sorry, ma'am." He headed toward the patio, but when he saw Julia conversing with his mother at the table, something shifted in his gut. He pivoted around and walked straight out of the hospital doors.

He needed some air.

* * *

Julia sat by Laney's bedside, holding her hand. To her immense relief, Laney's eyes were bright and she had color in her face. They'd gotten the news at four in the afternoon that mother and unborn baby were out of the woods. "You gave us quite a scare, honey."

"I'm sorry. It all happened so fast. Evan told me you've been here since last night. Thank you. I'll never forget that."

"I couldn't be anywhere else. I *had* to come. You look good, but how are you feeling?"

"Like I ran a fifty-mile marathon," she replied with a soft laugh. "But all that matters is that the baby is fine. Strong heartbeat again and no more contractions."

"That's the best news."

She nodded, patting her stomach. "The baby's grounded me though. I'll be confined to bed rest, at least for now. But I'm grateful, so no complaints. The medical staff has been terrific."

"Yeah, Evan kept them on their toes. No one slouched off while his wife was in trouble."

"Tyler men are like that," Lancy said, her voice filled with pride.

"Tell me about it."

Laney gave a little tilt of her head, her hair brushing against the pillow on her bed. "Have you and Trent gotten closer?"

"Depends on what you mean by closer?"

"I mean," Laney said, lowering her voice, but speaking passionately, "are you two in love?"

Julia closed her eyes tight and reopened them to face her good friend, who waited with a hopeful expression. "I am. Desperately. But Trent doesn't talk about his emotions. I'm taking it one day at a time with him. I don't think…I mean…I don't know what the future holds for us."

"Oh, Jules, that man has rocks in his head."

"Hard, granite rocks," she agreed.

"He should be bowing at your feet. According to Evan, you're the best thing that's ever happened to him."

"I've always liked Evan. He's a smart man," she mused, before coming to her lover's defense. "Trent's been really great since this all happened. I'll admit I was pretty shaken yesterday when I heard about you and the baby. Trent took control. He eased my mind and comforted me and always seemed to say the right things. He's been caring and sweet. It's a side to him I've not seen before and I like it very much."

"Maybe now's the time for you to make a stand, honey." Laney's face twisted. "Give him something to think about."

"Oh, Laney, please don't worry about me. I'm fine." Then she smiled, refusing to cause Laney a moment of anxiety about her love life of all things. She shifted the conversation. "I'm excited about the progress at Tempest West."

Julia spent the next twenty minutes speaking with

Laney about Sarah Rose and Ken Yellowhawk and all the things she'd planned for the hotel, until Evan walked into the room with Trent. Shortly after, Rebecca and her father joined them.

Julia slipped out to give them a chance to visit, and ten minutes later Trent met up with her in the waiting room, sidling up next to her by the window.

"She looks good," he said.

Julia nodded. "Thank heaven. She'll be confined to bed rest for a while, but she's fine with that as long as the baby continues to thrive."

"I'd better head back to Arizona. There's nothing more I can do here. Are you coming with me?"

Julia made up her mind hours ago that she wouldn't leave Laney. She'd promised Evan she'd stay a while to keep her company and help out when she came home from the hospital. "No, I'm staying a few days in L.A. to be with Laney."

Trent stared at her, then nodded and she couldn't quite read his expression. "Okay. Walk outside with me? A car is picking me up to take me to the airfield."

"I can do that," she said, and when Trent took hold of her hand and squeezed gently, her heart melted. Maybe his head was filled with rocks, but he'd been her *rock*, the solid ground she could tread upon when the world had gotten shaky. There was something valuable in that. She ached for him to admit his feelings for her, yet she couldn't deny that he'd been wonderful during the past twenty-four hours. He'd held her, comforted her and had been the moral support she'd needed. She doubted Trent had spent a night in bed just holding a woman before, to help her sleep. But he had done that for her.

And this morning, he'd taken charge, easing everyone's minds, distracting them all with a delicious catered breakfast.

She walked outside, squinting into the sunlight, side by side with Trent. He stopped by the sidewalk and she faced him, her hand shielding her eyes from the blistering sunshine, and spoke from her heart. "I don't know what I would have done without you, Trent. I think you know how frightened I was. But you held me up. You've been so solid in all this. Today, you were wonderful to everyone, seeing to all our needs." She smiled wide, looking into his deep dark appreciative eyes and felt a real twinge of hope. "I just wanted to thank you, before you left."

Trent took her into his strong embrace, his arms wrapping tightly around her waist. "Darlin', don't you know that I'd do anything to keep you at Tempest West."

He crushed his lips to her mouth, stroking her tongue and sweeping her into a storm of desire, right there in broad daylight.

The limousine pulled up right on schedule and Trent released her and smiled, before bounding into the car and driving off.

Julia caught her breath a second.

Before the true meaning of Trent's declaration struck her right between the eyes.

Eleven

Three days later, Julia returned to Tempest West and headed straight toward Trent's office. She wanted to get this over with once and for all. She wouldn't let the sight of him distract her from her mission. She'd fumed. She'd cried. She'd gone over and over it in her head dozens of times back in Los Angeles, but the bottom line had always been the same. The hardest part had been hiding from Laney that her brother-in-law had crushed her heart. Heaven knew that her friend didn't need any more worry after the fright she'd had with the baby. Laney's blood pressure was stabilized and Julia wanted to keep it that way.

After Trent left L.A., Julia hadn't taken his calls.

Anything work-related, she'd e-mailed straight back to Kim. She wanted nothing to keep her from her decision.

When she reached Trent's office, she stopped and inhaled sharply. She knew he was in there—he always arrived early in the morning before the rest of the staff.

Julia burst through the door, startling Trent. He lifted his head from the work he'd been concentrating on and raised his brows, before casting her a big smile. "Julia, I've been trying—"

"I'm resigning," she said, walking toward his desk and tossing her letter of resignation down in front of him. "I'll stay on for three weeks, until Sarah Rose leaves. But then I'm gone."

Trent rose abruptly. "What?"

"You heard me." She held her voice steady. "I want out, the sooner the better."

"What's got your panties in a knot, darlin'?"

He had. He'd gotten her panties in a knot, so much so, that she couldn't see what was right before her eyes. Trent was using her to gain ground with Tempest West, but he had no true feelings for her. He'd never said so. And what made her most angry was that she allowed it to happen. She'd been charmed right *out* of her panties.

"I'm through at Tempest West, Trent. You don't need me anymore. Your hotel is booked to capacity now. I've seen to that. My job is done here."

Trent appeared confused. His face contorted and he shook his head, raising his voice. "You're gone for three days. You don't answer my calls. I miss the hell out of you, and then you come back to say you're quitting? What the hell's going on?"

Julia lost him after he said he'd missed the hell out of her. But she couldn't believe him. She wasn't that big a fool. "You missed me? What did you miss, Trent? Me—making your life easy? Me—getting your precious hotel out of the red? Me—under your sheets at night? Or me? Just me?"

Trent stared at her, wordless.

Julia had her answer then. "I'm staying on for three weeks, not for your sake, Trent. I'm doing this for Sarah. I promised her I'd be here with her. I'll speak with you about hotel business, because after all, that's what you're paying me for, right? But don't ever approach me about anything else. Got that, boss?"

Trent came around his desk, slow and easy, marking his steps, and banking his fury, *just barely,* under the surface. "Why, Julia? Why are you doing this?"

She laughed softly, the absurdity hitting her.

Because you refuse to love me.

"You used me, Trent. And what's sad is that you don't even know that you've done it. You don't care about anything but your precious hotel. It's all that matters to you. I'm through living that way," she said with finality.

His nostrils flared and he spoke with authority, "Are you forgetting that I've got you under contract?"

"You don't have me *under* anything, anymore." She smiled, glad to have made that abundantly clear.

A tic worked in Trent's jaw, but the slight flicker in his eyes gave him away. "I could—"

"Sue me? Ruin my reputation? Go ahead and try. I'm not afraid of anything you might do. Any employer worth his salt would love to hire me. I have an impeccable reputation and a strong work ethic. My successes speak for themselves."

Trent scrubbed the back of his neck. He spoke softly now, perhaps realizing that she meant business. "Julia, come on. You're angry about something, but I can't figure it out. Just tell me what I did and I'll fix it."

Julia shook her head. "You don't get it. You can't fix this. You're a fool, Trent. But I'm the bigger fool. I fell in love with you."

Julia turned and walked away before witnessing Trent's reaction. She didn't want to see it. She couldn't bear to glimpse his stunned surprise or, worse yet, his indifference.

"Julia did a nice job setting this all up," Pete Wyatt said, as he sidled next to Trent and watched the hotel guests take their seats and eagerly await Sarah Rose to arrive. Trent leaned against a cottonwood tree in the background, arms folded, taking it all in.

There wasn't an empty seat to be had. Every single one of the invited guests was in attendance for this special private performance. Sarah Rose's signature background music played softly, getting the audience in the mood. Destiny Lake's dock had been transformed into a stage, surrounded by flowers and shrubbery that were native to Crimson Canyon.

"She did," Trent agreed, eyeing her from a distance as she made last-minute preparations by the dock. He had to give her credit. Julia had the ideas and the know-how to make things happen.

She looked so pretty in her country duds. She wore a denim skirt that fit her slim waist and a russet ruffled blouse that brought out her olive skin tones. She'd dressed for the special occasion, boots and all.

A knot formed in the pit of his stomach. Julia wasn't speaking to him. He'd gotten an earful from Evan and Brock today. News traveled fast in the Tyler clan and they all knew Julia had decided to leave Tempest West. He'd avoided the calls from his mother, though. He wasn't up to explaining something to her that he couldn't explain to himself.

Julia took a stand on the dock facing the crowd, her face alight with anticipation and…pride. She glanced out at the guests and the background music ceased playing. She spoke to the group, welcoming them to Tempest West's first exclusive performance, and was greeted with a round of applause. When the applause died down, Julia began, "As you know, Tempest West is all about legends. Live our legends or create one of your own. So before we get started, I'd like to tell you how this beautiful lake got its name and about the struggles, hopes and dreams of the people who lived here decades ago and witnessed this amazing canyon sunset every day of their lives. The legend goes…."

Julia spoke from the heart, emotion ringing out in every word. When she was through telling the tale, she introduced Sarah Rose and turned her attention out on the waters. The country singer appeared in a boat on the shimmering lake, being rowed toward the dock by two Tempest West wranglers. She waved to her audience and they cheered as she was helped up the few landing steps and handed her guitar.

Sarah sat on the stool placed on the edge of the dock and began to sing, the orange-gold sun setting behind her, streaking vivid hues of color across the lake.

Brilliant.

The guests loved it.

Trent glanced at Julia, and she turned to him at the same time from yards away, their eyes meeting and for one second there was triumph and bonding—they'd accomplished their goal together. But then, the spark in her eyes went dim. Trent winced at the extreme sadness he witnessed on her face before she turned away.

Suddenly, Trent feared losing something more precious than his hotel. Julia loved him. He didn't have to search his heart far to know he'd blown it with her, big-time. Evan and Brock had both told him so, tossing in a few expletives along the way, the phone conversations not the highlight of his day. He'd let his own ambition and drive blind him and now it was too late.

"You got a new head wrangler in mind yet?" Pete asked quietly.

The question broke into his thoughts. Trent nodded. "I think Joe Hardy can do the job."

Pete agreed. "He's a good man."

"You sure you want to leave?"

Pete sighed and shook his head. "It's time I go back home. Things here got more complicated than I thought."

"Female trouble?"

"Yeah, and I don't need more of it. I appreciate you keeping my secret," he said. "I owe you one."

Trent smiled at his friend. "I know where to find you."

Pete nodded and they both stood there, listening to Sarah Rose's sweet stirrings in a soft sad ballad of unrequited love.

"You're leaving," Kim said to Julia, her heartache evident on her face.

Nothing much got by the watercooler gang. Tempest West was like a small city in itself and it seemed everyone knew the score. Julia gazed at her new friend as they walked toward the hotel for the postshow party in honor of Sarah's first performance. Julia knew how much she'd miss the young impulsive girl.

There were a dozen things she'd miss about Tempest West. She'd made friends here. She'd enjoyed the work, the challenge and the gorgeous surroundings. Her vision for Tempest West was beginning, but she wouldn't have the pleasure of seeing it through.

Sarah's concert was the first step and it had been hugely successful.

She put her arm around Kim as they headed for the Canyon Room.

"It's going to be hard without you here, Julia."

Julia felt the same way. She'd miss her newfound friendship with Kim. But she had to leave. She couldn't get past her hurt and anger at Trent. She hadn't spoken more than a few sentences to him in the past few days. "You know we'll always be friends."

"I hope so," she said.

"We'll talk more about this tomorrow. Now, let's go tell Sarah how wonderful her performance was." They climbed the stone steps that led to the back lobby entrance and entered the restaurant for the party. "I think she could use a friend tonight, too."

"Yes," Kim said, perking up a little bit, "the girls need to stick together."

Julia saw Code Landon leaning against the fireplace watching Sarah with eagle eyes as she spoke with a young newlywed couple. She and Kim moved toward her and after she'd finished signing an autograph, Julia and Kim approached. Julia took Sarah's arm and once they reached a quiet corner of the room, she hugged Sarah tight. "Thank you," she whispered. "You were wonderful."

"You were, Sarah. Everyone enjoyed your show," Kim said.

"I enjoyed doing it more than you can imagine,"

Sarah said, her voice laced with gratitude. "I'd almost forgotten what it was like playing to a small audience. I feel like we can really connect with the music together." She took a breath and continued, "You know, I've always thought I knew what I wanted from life." She glanced Code's way with a flicker of regret in her eyes. "But sometimes, when we're young, we don't always have it right."

"Ain't that the truth," Kim acknowledged.

Julia laughed softly, until she turned and saw Trent standing next to Code by the massive fireplace. Two handsome men with two sets of eyes directed to their little female group. Her heart plummeted and she felt overwhelming sadness consume her.

A waiter passed by holding a tray of bubbling champagne flutes. Julia stopped him and handed each woman a glass. "Let's toast," she said, clicking the tip of her flute to the others. "To you, Sarah, for bringing your incredible talent here to Tempest West and to you, Kim, my new friend. Ladies, here's to getting it right in the future."

The women repeated the sentiment and sipped champagne, Julia acknowledging that each one of them hid certain tender sorrows behind their smiling faces.

Two hours later, Sarah excused herself from the party flanked by hotel security in plain clothes, and the partygoers dwindled rapidly. Julia stayed on to speak with the staff on strategies to make the next performance go even smoother. "Okay, thank you," she said, closing her notebook and dismissing them from the table. They all rose together. "You all did a terrific job."

"So did you." The voice came from behind and she whirled around to find Trent standing nearby. She glanced at the staff members, who had scurried off in different directions, and found herself alone with Trent in the Canyon Room.

"Just doing my job," she replied, not ready for a confrontation. She hugged the notebook to her chest and began walking away.

"You're walking out? I'm trying to thank you, Julia."

"Consider it done," she said, facing him directly. That tic worked his jawline again.

"I'm not through yet."

"Well, hell. I don't think I care." She caught herself and refused to argue. The fight was all out of her anyway. "I'm exhausted, Trent. I need to get some sleep."

"Julia, listen. I've got things I need to say to you."

Trent held his ground and spoke with determination, but there was nothing he could say to her now. She didn't trust him. Had never really trusted him. He'd given her no reason to. "Is it business?" she asked.

"Hell, no!" He approached her, taking steps her way.

"Well, then, I'm sorry. But there's nothing that I want to hear from you. I thought I made that clear the other day."

Trent pursed his lips. His face flamed and his body grew rigid. She'd angered him, but it was the only way she knew to keep him from approaching her, hurting her even more.

She sidestepped him, accidentally brushing his shoulder, and walked straight out of the room.

Leaving a good chunk of her heart behind.

Two days later, Julia lay on her bed, her head on her pillow, gazing out the window. Morning sunlight cast Crimson Canyon in lush shades of gold, a stunning view she'd come to anticipate each day and one she'd miss once she left here. Just a few more weeks and she'd be gone.

She let go a big dramatic sigh, her emotions in turmoil. She'd spent half the night crying and the other half cursing Trent, his stubbornness and her own stupidity for falling for him. She'd never experienced such shattering pain before, but she was proud that she had stood up for herself. She'd be able to leave here holding her head high, fully satisfied with her accomplishments, knowing her efforts would leave Tempest West headed in the right direction.

When her cell phone rang, Julia listened to the musical tune for a few seconds. She wasn't in the mood to speak with anyone really but the caller was persistent. She checked the number. It was her father. She'd told him yesterday that she was leaving her job earlier than expected and he'd pried more information out of her than she'd wanted to divulge. No doubt, he was worried about her. Daughter guilt sunk in and she answered in a cheerful voice. "Hi, Dad."

"Hi, baby. How are you?"

"I've been better, frankly. But I'll be okay."

Her father laughed sympathetically. "Want me to come over and punch that cowboy's lights out for you?"

"Dad!" It sounded too much like a good idea.

"Ah, Julia…I'm sorry it didn't work out for you. But sometimes, it's all for the best. You just gotta have faith."

"I know, Dad. And I do," she fibbed, curious at her father's optimism. "I'll be home soon and then I'll… regroup. I've got some other job prospects that I'm looking into."

"That's good, Julia. I know my little girl will find happiness soon."

Julia didn't have any such hopes, so she remained silent.

Her father continued, "I have something to tell you and I hope my timing isn't way off. I don't want to cause you any…well, more unhappiness, but I also don't want you to hear this from anyone but me. The fact is, that Rebecca Tyler and I are going to start seeing each other seriously."

Julia closed her eyes. She couldn't be anything but happy for her father. She'd known all along he'd been lonely lately, and Rebecca Tyler was a sweet caring woman, but, oh…that was just one more way she'd be tied to Trent. "Rebecca's a lovely woman, Dad," she responded, after a long silence. "I'm happy for you, but a long-distance romance? Won't that be hard on you?"

"No, I'm more concerned about it being *hard* on you."

"Don't worry about me, Dad. I'll be working somewhere else soon, and I think I can put everything in perspective. You deserve to be happy."

"Thank you, honey. So you're okay with it?"

"Yes, Dad. I'm fine with it," she said sincerely. She'd just have to deal with Laney being married to Trent's brother and her father seeing Trent's mother. She didn't have much choice anyway. "I can see that you and Rebecca are very…compatible."

Her father laughed again. "Compatible? Honey, that's such an old-fashioned word. We're *hot* for each other."

"Dad!"

He continued to chuckle, his voice light. "We may be senior citizens but we've still got some mileage left. I have the utmost respect for Rebecca. She's going to stay at Evan's hotel in L.A. for a while to be near Laney and help out. And I'll go to Florida for visits. I think it'll work."

"Then I'm happy for you. Really."

"Thank you, honey."

After the phone call, Julia rose from bed and decided to take a long soak in the tub. It was Sunday and she didn't have to work today. Sarah's weekend performances had gone like clockwork with no problems or issues and the hotel had never been busier. Every venue was being utilized to maximum capacity, the gift shops and restaurants flourished and the stables' guided tours were booked. During the week, Ken Yellowhawk would begin his series of southwest art lectures and instruction up on Shadow Ridge. And Julia had already booked another singer for Tempest West who agreed to stay on for six weeks.

Julia stripped off her silk pajamas and headed for the

bathroom, ready to start her bath, but another cell phone call interrupted. "Oh, for heaven's sake," she said, wrapping a towel around her, inclined not to answer. But again she looked at the caller ID and picked up. "Hi, Sarah."

"Good morning, Julia. I hope I'm not disturbing you."

"Not at all," she fibbed again, and wondered wryly if they gave out an award for fibbing. "I'm not doing anything."

"Oh, that's good," she said with relief. "Remember when you offered to speak with me about…well, my relationship with Code?"

"Yes, and the offer still stands."

"I hate to ask this of you…but could you give me some of your time this morning? I, uh…need to speak with you. Something's come up."

Sarah seemed so hesitant and Julia wanted to ease her mind. "Of course, Sarah. I'll be glad to talk to you. Just give me half an hour to shower and dress. I can be over to your—"

"Can you meet me at the lake? I need…I need some fresh air. I'll be on the dock."

She frowned. Sarah sounded very upset and Julia had always known there was more to Sarah's childhood friendship with Code than she let on. She only hoped that he hadn't compromised her stay at Tempest West. "I'll be there in thirty minutes tops."

Sarah's voice lifted. "Oh, thank you. And, Julia, I hope you know I think of you as a good friend."

"I do know that. I feel the same way. I'll see you in a few."

Julia showered quickly, dressed in her faded jeans, threw on a Phoenix Suns T-shirt Kim had given her and slipped on her leather boots. She pulled her hair back in a ponytail and walked out the door twenty-two minutes later. What Sarah had to say had to be important and she didn't want to be late, giving her a chance to chicken out. Whatever it was, she'd seemed awfully tentative on the phone. At least, Julia thought, helping Sarah with a dilemma would take her mind off her own heartache.

Julia reached the dock first and was glad that there weren't a lot of people around. Most of the guests were at the Sunday morning brunch held on the patio and in the Canyon Room. Julia stood looking out at Destiny Lake, a slight cool breeze reminding her that there would soon be colder weather.

The view here was breathtaking with deep blue waters glimmering and Crimson Canyon catching daylight. Julia took a big breath and swallowed, thinking of the windowless corporate offices she'd face when she returned home.

She heard footsteps approach and spun around, expecting to see Sarah.

Trent stood on the dock facing her, wearing an ink-black tuxedo, a string tie and brand-new shining boots. She struggled to keep her jaw from dropping. Then she blinked.

Trent smiled and her heart fluttered.

"Hello, Julia."

Stunned, Julia nodded her greeting. Trent looked like a zillion bucks, and then some. She couldn't let that sway her, but she was curious why he was so duded up, as the cowboys say. "I'm meeting Sarah here and we'll need privacy."

Trent sighed. "No, you're not. Sarah's not coming. And she says she's sorry."

Julia blinked again, confused. "What do you mean?"

"I put her up to it. She called you on my behalf."

Julia should be angry, but it was difficult getting angry with a man who looked better than a hot-fudge sundae with whipped cream and cherries. "Why?"

Trent moved closer and took her hand in his. He brought it to his lips and kissed her fingertips. His dark eyes fastened to hers. "Because I love you. And I needed you to know that, darlin'."

A surge of warmth spread through her body. "You love me?"

"I do, Julia. With all my heart."

Julia wanted to believe him, but Trent had never offered up his love before. How could she trust that he wasn't just making the declaration to keep her at Tempest West?

"I'm asking you to marry me, Julia. Be my wife. Have my children."

Hope skipped along her heart. "Oh, Trent."

He reached into his pocket and produced a ring box. He opened it and a brilliant pink marquis diamond ring reflected against the morning light. Julia's mouth dropped open this time, but she couldn't quite find the words.

Trent searched her face for her answer. Stunned into silence, her mouth refused to work. Then he reached into his jacket and lifted out a folded document. He handed it to her. "My love and the ring, goes along with this."

Julia glanced down and read the words *prenuptial agreement*.

A frown pulled her lips down and tears stung her eyes. Trent hadn't changed at all. He wanted her on his terms and he'd even resort to offer her marriage, to keep her at Tempest West.

Her body trembled uncontrollably and she fought humiliation, allowing anger to take its place. "How dare you, Trent Tyler? You don't know me at all! You think a woman wants a contract for a proposal? You think I don't know that you'd do anything for this hotel. You don't love me. I'm your ticket to success, that's all!" She flung her arms up in the air, spun on her heels and walked away before she made a bigger scene, crumpling the document in her hand as she stalked off.

"Wait!" Trent commanded and Julia stopped at the edge of the dock. "Read it, sweetheart. Read it and know I mean every word."

There was something in Trent's tone, something soft and pleading that broke into her anger. Still shaking, she unfolded the paper and read through the wrinkled paper.

Darlin',
This is to certify that I love you deeply. It's my fondest wish that you become my wife, mother of

my children, partner of my heart and all my assets, but you are under no obligation to ever work for me again…unless it's your desire.

I love you more than anything else in life. Julia, you are my miracle.

Trent

Julia turned and Trent was there, facing her. Tears of joy streamed down her face now as she looked into his eyes and saw the truth there. God, how she loved him. She opened her heart and trust poured inside. Finally, she believed him. He loved her. "You really do mean this?"

He nodded and took her into his arms. "Every word. I love you, Julia. I can't imagine my life without you."

"Oh, Trent. I love you, too. Very much."

"Then you'll marry me?"

She nodded. "Yes. I'll marry you."

"Good," Trent said, placing the ring on her finger. "Your father said you would, but I had my doubts—"

"My father?"

"I called him last night and asked for your hand."

"You did?" That explained her father's sudden optimism. The phone call wasn't only about Rebecca. He'd known about Trent's intentions when they spoke this morning. She smiled happily. "I'm impressed."

"I hope to spend my life *impressing* you."

"I look forward to that, sweetheart," she said, snuggling in his arms.

Trent bent his head and took her in a kiss that spoke

of promise and love and a future filled with joy. Then he wrapped his arms around her shoulders and turned her to face the glistening water.

As they looked out at Destiny Lake, he said quietly, "We were given a second chance in life, just like the legend says. We've lived the legend."

Julia leaned against Trent and sighed. "And now we'll create one of our own."

She would spend her life loving her own five-star cowboy.

And that was truly a miracle.

* * * * *

Don't miss
DO NOT DISTURB UNTIL CHRISTMAS,
Charlene's next book in SUITE SECRETS,
available November 2008 from
Silhouette Desire.

The Colton family is back!
Enjoy a sneak preview of
COLTON'S SECRET SERVICE
by Marie Ferrarella, part of
THE COLTONS: FAMILY FIRST *miniseries.*
Available from Silhouette Romantic Suspense
in September 2008.

He cautioned himself to be leery. He was human and he'd been conned before. But never by anyone nearly so attractive. Never by anyone he'd felt so attracted to.

In her defense, Nick supposed that Georgie could actually be telling him the truth. That she was a victim in all this. He had his people back in California checking her out, to make sure she was who she said she was and had, as she claimed, not even been near a computer but on the road these last few months that the threats had been made.

In the meantime, he was doing his own checking out. Up close and exceedingly personal. So personal he could feel his blood stirring.

It had been a long time since he'd thought of himself

as anything other than a law enforcement agent of one type or other. But Georgeann Grady made him remember that beneath the oaths he had taken and his devotion to duty, there beat the heart of a man.

A man who'd been far too long without the touch of a woman.

He watched as the light from the fireplace caressed the outline of Georgie's small, trim, jean-clad body as she moved about the rustic living room that could have easily come off the set of a Hollywood Western. Except that it was genuine.

As genuine as she claimed to be?

Something inside of him hoped so.

He wasn't supposed to be taking sides. His only interest in being here was to guarantee Senator Joe Colton's safety as the latter continued to make his bid for the presidency. Everything else was supposed to be secondary, but, Nick had to silently admit, that was just a wee bit hard to remember right now.

Earlier, before she'd put her precocious handful of a daughter to bed, Georgie had fed his appetite by whipping up some kind of a delicious concoction out of the vegetables she'd pulled from her garden. Vegetables that, by all rights, should have been withered and dried. She'd mentioned that a friend came by on occasion to weed and tend it. Still, it surprised him that somehow she'd managed to make something mouthwatering out of it.

Almost as mouthwatering as she looked to him right at this moment.

Again, he was reminded of the appetite that hadn't been fed, hadn't been satisfied.

And wasn't going to be, Nick sternly told himself. At least not now. Maybe later, when things took on a more definite shape and all the questions in his head were answered to his satisfaction, there would be time to explore this feeling. This woman. But not now.

Damn it.

"Sorry about the lack of light," Georgie said, breaking into his train of thought as she turned around to face him. If she noticed the way he was looking at her, she gave no indication. "But I don't see a point in paying for electricity if I'm not going to be here. Besides, Emmie really enjoys camping out. She likes roughing it."

"And you?" Nick asked, moving closer to her, so close that a whisper would have trouble fitting in. "What do you like?"

The very breath stopped in Georgie's throat as she looked up at him.

"I think you've got a fair shot of guessing that one," she told him softly.

* * * * *

Be sure to look for COLTON'S SECRET SERVICE
and the other following titles from
THE COLTONS: FAMILY FIRST *miniseries:*
RANCHER'S REDEMPTION
by Beth Cornelison
THE SHERIFF'S AMNESIAC BRIDE
by Linda Conrad
SOLDIER'S SECRET CHILD by Caridad Piñeiro
BABY'S WATCH by Justine Davis
A HERO OF HER OWN by Carla Cassidy

Silhouette®

Romantic
SUSPENSE

**Sparked by Danger,
Fueled by Passion.**

The Coltons Are Back!

Marie Ferrarella
Colton's Secret Service

The Coltons: Family First

On a mission to protect a senator, Secret Service agent
Nick Sheffield tracks down a threatening message only
to discover Georgie Gradie Colton, a rodeo-riding single
mom, who insists on her innocence. Nick is instantly
taken with the feisty redhead, but vows not to let his
feelings interfere with his mission. Now he must figure
out if this woman is conning him or if he can trust her
and the passion they share....

Available September wherever books are sold.

**Look for upcoming Colton titles
from Silhouette Romantic Suspense:**

RANCHER'S REDEMPTION by Beth Cornelison, Available October
THE SHERIFF'S AMNESIAC BRIDE by Linda Conrad, Available November
SOLDIER'S SECRET CHILD by Caridad Piñeiro, Available December
BABY'S WATCH by Justine Davis, Available January 2009
A HERO OF HER OWN by Carla Cassidy, Available February 2009

Visit Silhouette Books at www.eHarlequin.com   SRS27598

Silhouette Desire

Billionaires and Babies

MAUREEN CHILD

BABY BONANZA

Newly single mom Jenna Baker has only one thing on her mind: child support for her twin boys. Ship owner and carefree billionaire Nick Falco discovers he's a daddy—brought on by a night of passion a year ago. Nick may be ready to become a father, but is he ready to become a groom when he discovers the passion that still exists between him and Jenna?

**Available September
wherever books are sold.**

Always Powerful, Passionate and Provocative.

REQUEST YOUR FREE BOOKS!

2 FREE NOVELS PLUS 2 FREE GIFTS!

Passionate, Powerful, Provocative!

YES! Please send me 2 FREE Silhouette Desire® novels and my 2 FREE gifts (gifts are worth about $10). After receiving them, if I don't wish to receive any more books, I can return the shipping statement marked "cancel". If I don't cancel, I will receive 6 brand-new novels every month and be billed just $4.05 per book in the U.S. or $4.74 per book in Canada, plus 25¢ shipping and handling per book and applicable taxes, if any*. That's a savings of almost 15% off the cover price! I understand that accepting the 2 free books and gifts places me under no obligation to buy anything. I can always return a shipment and cancel at any time. Even if I never buy another book, the two free books and gifts are mine to keep forever.

225 SDN ERVX 326 SDN ERVM

Name	(PLEASE PRINT)	
Address		Apt. #
City	State/Prov.	Zip/Postal Code

Signature (if under 18, a parent or guardian must sign)

Mail to the Silhouette Reader Service:
IN U.S.A.: P.O. Box 1867, Buffalo, NY 14240-1867
IN CANADA: P.O. Box 609, Fort Erie, Ontario L2A 5X3

Not valid to current subscribers of Silhouette Desire books.

Want to try two free books from another line?
Call 1-800-873-8635 or visit www.morefreebooks.com.

* Terms and prices subject to change without notice. N.Y. residents add applicable sales tax. Canadian residents will be charged applicable provincial taxes and GST. Offer not valid in Quebec. This offer is limited to one order per household. All orders subject to approval. Credit or debit balances in a customer's account(s) may be offset by any other outstanding balance owed by or to the customer. Please allow 4 to 6 weeks for delivery. Offer available while quantities last.

Your Privacy: Silhouette Books is committed to protecting your privacy. Our Privacy Policy is available online at www.eHarlequin.com or upon request from the Reader Service. From time to time we make our lists of customers available to reputable third parties who may have a product or service of interest to you. If you would prefer we not share your name and address, please check here. ☐

SDES08R

Silhouette Desire

COMING NEXT MONTH

#1891 PRINCE OF MIDTOWN—Jennifer Lewis
Park Avenue Scandals
This royal had only one way to keep his dedicated—and lovely—
assistant under his roof...seduce her into his bed!

#1892 THE M.D.'S MISTRESS—Joan Hohl
Gifts from a Billionaire
Finally she was with the sexy surgeon she'd always loved. But
would their affair last longer than the week?

#1893 BABY BONANZA—Maureen Child
Billionaires and Babies
Secret twin babies? A carefree billionaire discovers he's a
daddy—but is he ready to become a groom?

#1894 WED BY DECEPTION—Emilie Rose
The Payback Affairs
The husband she'd believed dead was back—and very much alive.
And determined to make her his...at any cost.

#1895 HIS EXPECTANT EX—Catherine Mann
The Landis Brothers
The ink was not yet dry on their divorce papers when she
discovered she was pregnant. Could a baby bring them a second
chance?

#1896 THE DESERT KING—Olivia Gates
Throne of Judar
Forced to marry to save his throne, this desert king could not deny
the passion he felt for his bride of *in*convenience.

SDCNM0808